Memoirs of a Space Traveler

Also by Stanislaw Lem

MEMOIRS OF A SPACE TRAVELER

Further Reminiscences of Ijon Tichy

STANISLAW LEM

Drawings by the Author

Translated by Joel Stern and Maria Swiecicka-Ziemianek

A Helen and Kurt Wolff Book

Harcourt Brace Jovanovich, Publishers

New York and London

Requests for permission to make copies
of any part of the work should be mailed to:
Permissions, Harcourt Brace Jovanovich, Inc.,
757 Third Avenue, New York, N.Y. 10017

The following originally appeared in *The New Yorker:*
"The Eighteenth Voyage," "The Twenty-fourth Voyage,"
"The Washing Machine Tragedy," and "Let Us Save the Universe."

Library of Congress Cataloging in Publication Data

Lem, Stanislaw.
Memoirs of a space traveler.

Translation of: Dzienniki gwiazdowe. 1971.
"A Helen and Kurt Wolff book."
Contents: The eighteenth voyage—
The twenty-fourth voyage—
Further reminiscences of Ijon Tichy—[etc.]
I. Title.
PG7158.L39D9132   1982   891.8'537   81-47310
ISBN 0-15-158856-2   AACR2

Printed in the United States of America

First edition

B C D E

PUBLISHER'S NOTE

The pieces in this book—the two Voyages of Ijon Tichy, his reminiscences, his open letter—all appeared in the 1971 Polish edition of *Dzienniki gwiazdowe* (*The Star Diaries*) but were not included in the British and American editions titled *The Star Diaries* and published in 1976. The present book, in effect, constitutes the second volume of Lem's work of that name.

Contents

Memoirs of a Space Traveler

The Eighteenth Voyage

The expedition I want to write about now was, in its consequences and scale, the greatest of my life. I am well aware that no one will believe me. But, paradoxical as it may seem, the Reader's disbelief will facilitate my task. Because I cannot claim that I achieved what I intended to achieve. To tell the truth, the whole thing turned out rather badly. The fact that it was not I who bungled, but certain envious and ignorant people who tried to thwart my plans, does not ease my conscience any.

So, then, the goal of this expedition was the creation of the Universe. Not some new, separate universe, one that never before existed. No. I mean this Universe we live in. On the face of it, an absurd, an insane statement, for how can one create what exists already and what is as ancient and irreversible as the Universe? Could this be—the Reader is likely to think—a wild hypothesis stating that till now nothing has existed except Earth, and that all the galaxies, suns, stellar clouds, and Milky Ways are only a mirage? But that's not it at all, because I really did create everything, absolutely Everything—and thus Earth, too, and the rest of the Solar System, and the Metagalaxy, which would certainly be cause for pride, if only my handiwork did not contain so many flaws. Some of these lie in the building material, but most are in the animate matter, particularly in the human race. This has been my greatest regret. True, the people I shall mention by name interfered in my efforts, but by no means do I consider myself thereby absolved. I should have planned, supervised, seen to everything more carefully. Especially since there is now no possibility for correction or improvement. Since October 20 of last year, I am to blame for all—and I mean all—the constructional defects in the Universe and the warps in human nature. There is no escape from that knowledge.

It all began three years ago, when through Professor Tarantoga I met a certain physicist of Slavic descent from Bombay. A visiting professor. This scientist, Solon Razglaz, had spent thirty years in the study of cosmogony, that branch of astronomy that deals with the origin and early formation of the Universe.

Razglaz reached, after a thorough study of the subject, a conclusion that stunned even him. As we know, theories of cosmogony can be divided into two groups. One comprises those theories that regard the Universe as eternal—in other words, devoid of a beginning. The second holds that at one time the Universe arose in a violent manner, from the explosion of a Proto-atom. There have always been difficulties with both views. Regarding the first: Science possesses a growing body of evidence that the visible Universe is from twelve to twenty billion years old. If something has a definite age, there is nothing simpler than to calculate back to its zero moment. But an eternal Universe can have no "zero," no beginning. Under the pressure of new information, most scientists now opt for a Universe that arose from fifteen to eighteen billion years ago. Initially there was a substance—call it Ylem, the Proto-atom, whatever—that exploded and gave rise to matter and energy, stellar clouds, spiral galaxies, and dark and bright nebulae, all floating in rarefied gas filled with radiation. This can be precisely and neatly determined as long as no one asks, "But where did the Proto-atom come from?" For there is no answer to this question. There are certain evasions, yes, but no self-respecting astronomer is satisfied with them.

Professor Razglaz, before taking up cosmogony, had for a long time studied theoretical physics, particularly the so-called elementary particles. When his interest switched to the new subject, he quickly saw that the Universe unquestionably had a beginning. It obviously arose 18.5 billion years ago from a single Proto-atom. At the same time, however, the Proto-atom from which it sprang could not have existed. For who could have placed it in that emptiness? In the very beginning there was nothing. Had there been something, that something, it is clear, would have begun developing at once, and the entire Universe would have arisen much earlier—infinitely earlier, to be exact! Why should a primordial Proto-atom remain inert, waiting motionless for unknown eons? And what in God's name could have wrenched it so, in that one moment, causing it to expand and fly apart into something so tremendous?

Learning of Razglaz's theory, I often questioned him about what led to his discovery. The origin of great ideas has always fascinated me, and surely it would be hard to find a greater revelation than Razglaz's cosmogonic hypothesis! The professor, a quiet and extremely modest man, told me that his concept was, from the viewpoint of orthodox astronomy, quite outrageous. Every astronomer knows that the atomic seed from which the Universe is supposed to have sprung is a highly problematical thing. What do they do about this, then? They sidestep, they evade the issue, because it is

inconvenient. Razglaz, on the other hand, dared to devote all his energy to it. The more he amassed facts, and
the more he rummaged through libraries and built
models, surrounding himself with a battery of the fastest
computers, the more clearly he saw that there was something not right.

At first he hoped that eventually he would succeed in
diminishing the contradiction, and perhaps even in re-
solving it. However, it kept increasing. Because all the
data indicated that the Universe arose from a single
atom, but also that no such atom could have existed.
Here an obvious explanation suggested itself, the God
hypothesis, but Razglaz set it aside as a last resort.
I remember his smile when he said, "We shouldn't
pass the buck to God. Certainly an astrophysi-
cist shouldn't. . . ." Pondering the dilemma for many
months, Razglaz reviewed his previous research. Ask
any physicist you know, if you do not believe me, and he
will tell you that certain phenomena on the smallest
scale occur, as it were, on credit. Mesons, those elementary particles, sometimes violate the laws of conservation, but they do this so incredibly fast that they hardly
violate them at all. What is forbidden by the laws of
physics they do with lightning speed, as though nothing could be more natural, and then they immediately
submit to those laws again. And so, on one of his morning strolls across the university campus, Razglaz asked
himself: What if the Universe were doing the same thing
on a large scale? If mesons can behave impossibly for a
fraction of a second, a fraction so minuscule that a whole
second would seem an eternity in comparison, then the
Universe, given its dimensions, might behave in that
forbidden way for a correspondingly longer period of
time. For, say, fifteen billion years. . . .

It arose, then, although it might well have not arisen, *there being nothing from which to arise.* The Universe is a *forbidden fluctuation.* It represents a momentary aberration, but an aberration of monumental proportions. It is no less a deviation from the laws of physics than, on the smallest scale, a meson! Suspecting he was on the right track, the professor immediately went to his laboratory and made some calculations, which, step by step, verified his idea. But even before he had finished, the realization came: the solution to the riddle of the origin of the Universe revealed a threat as great as could be imagined.

For the Universe exists *on credit.* It represents, with its constellations and galaxies, a monstrous debt, a pawn ticket, as it were, a promissory note that must ultimately be paid. The Universe is an illegal loan of matter and energy; its apparent "asset" is actually a "liability." Since the Universe is an Unlawful Anomaly, it will, one fine day, burst like a bubble. It will fall back into the Nonexistence from which it sprang. That moment will be a return to the Natural Order of Things!

That the Universe is so vast and that so much has taken place in it is due solely to the fact that we are dealing with a fluke on the largest possible scale. Razglaz immediately proceeded to calculate when the fatal term would come, that is, when matter, the Sun, the stars, the planets, and therefore Earth, along with all of us, would plunge into nothingness as though snuffed out. He learned that it was impossible to predict this. Of course impossible, given that the Universe was a fluke, a deviation from order! The danger revealed by his discovery kept him awake at night. After much inner struggle, he chose not to publish his cosmogonic research, instead acquainting a few eminent astrophysicists with it. These scientists acknowledged the correctness of his theory and conclusions. At the same time, they felt that publication of his findings would plunge the world into spiritual chaos and alarm, the consequences of which could destroy civilization. What man would still desire to do anything—to move his little finger—knowing that at any second everything might vanish, himself included?

The matter came to a standstill. Razglaz, the greatest discoverer in all history, agreed with his learned colleagues. He decided, albeit reluctantly, not to publish his theory. Instead, he began searching the whole arsenal of physics for ways to assist the Universe somehow, to strengthen and maintain its debtor's life. But his efforts came to naught. It was impossible to cancel the cosmic debt by anything done in the present: the debt lay not within the Universe but at its origin—at that point in time when the Universe became the mightiest and yet most defenseless Debtor to Nothingness.

It was at this juncture that I met the professor and spent many weeks in conversations with him. First he outlined for me the essential points of his discovery; then we worked together to find some means of deliverance.

Ah—I thought, returning to my hotel with fevered head and despairing heart—if only I could have been there, twenty billion years ago, for just a split second! That would be enough to place a single solitary atom in the void, and the Universe could grow from it as from a planted seed, now in a totally legitimate way, in accordance with the laws of physics and the principle of conservation of matter and energy. But how was I to get there?

The professor, when I told him this idea, smiled sadly

and explained to me that the Universe could not have arisen from any ordinary atom; the cosmic nucleus would have had to contain the energy of all the transformations and events that expanded to fill the metagalactic void. I saw my error, but continued to mull over the problem. Then, one afternoon, as I rubbed oil on my legs, which were swollen with mosquito bites, my mind wandered back to the old days, when, while flying through the spherical cluster of Canes Venatici, I had read theoretical physics for lack of anything better to do. I had been particularly engrossed in a volume devoted to elementary particles, and I recalled Feynman's hypothesis that there are particles that move "upstream" against the flow of time. When an electron moves in this manner, we perceive it then as an electron with a positive charge (a positron). I asked myself, with my feet in a washbasin: What if we took one electron and accelerated it, accelerated it so much that it would begin moving backward in time, faster and faster? Couldn't we give it such a tremendous impulse that it would fly back beyond the beginning of cosmic time to that point when there was still nothing? Couldn't the Universe arise from this accelerated positron?!

I ran to the professor as I was, my bare feet dripping wet. He immediately realized the magnitude of my idea and without a word began to calculate. It turned out that the project was feasible: his calculations showed that the electron, as it moved against the flow of time, would gain greater and greater energy, so that when it reached beyond the beginning of the Universe, the force accumulated within it would split it apart, and the exploding particle would release the energy required to cancel the debt. The Universe then would be saved from collapse, since it would no longer exist on credit!

Now we had only to think about the practical side of the undertaking that was to legitimize the World or, in short, to create it! As a man of integrity, Razglaz repeatedly said to Professor Tarantoga and to all his assistants and colleagues that it was I who had originated the concept of the Creation; that therefore it was I, and not he, who deserved the double title of Creator and Saviour of the World. I mention this not to boast but to humble myself. Because the endless praise and appreciation that I received at that time in Bombay, well, I'm afraid it turned my head a little and caused me to neglect my work. I rested on my laurels, thinking that the most important part had been done—the intellectual part—and that what followed now would be the purely technical details, which others could take care of.

A fatal mistake! Throughout the summer and most of the fall, Razglaz and I determined the parameters, the characteristics and properties that were to be carried by the electron—the cosmic seed, or, perhaps more correctly, the constructional quantum. As for the mechanical aspect of Project Genesis, we took a huge university synchrophasetron and rebuilt it into a cannon aimed at the beginning of time. All its power, concentrated and focused in a single particle—the constructional quantum—was to be released on October 20. Professor Razglaz insisted that I, the author of the idea, fire the world-forming shot from the Chronocannon. Because, you see, this was a unique historical opportunity. Our machine, our mortar, was to shoot not just any random electron, but a particle suitably remade, reshaped, and remodeled to bring forth a *much more orderly and solid* Universe than the one that existed at present. And we paid particular attention to the *intermediate* and *late stages of Cosmocreation*—the human race!

Of course, to program and pack such an ungodly wealth of information into one electron was no easy task. I must confess that I did not do everything myself. Razglaz and I shared the work; I thought up the improvements and corrections, and he translated these into the precise language of the parameters of physics, the theory of vacuums, the theory of electrons, positrons, and sundry other trons. We also set up a kind of incubator where we kept test particles in strict isolation. We would choose from among them the most successful particle, which, as I said, was to give birth to the Universe on October 20.

What good, what wonderful things I planned during those hectic days! How often did I work late into the night poring over books on physics, ethics, and zoology in order to gather, combine, and concentrate the most valuable information, which the professor, starting at dawn, fashioned into the electron, the cosmic nucleus! We wanted, among other things, to have the Universe develop harmoniously, not as before; to prevent supernovas from jolting it too much; to eliminate the senseless waste of quasar and pulsar energy; to keep stars from sparking and smoking like damp candlewicks; and to shorten interstellar distances, which would facilitate space travel and thus bring together and unify sentient races. It would take volumes to tell of all the corrections I managed to plan in a relatively short time. But these were not the most important thing. I need not explain why I concentrated on the human race; to improve it, I changed the principle of natural evolution.

Evolution, as we know, is either the wholesale devouring of the weaker by the stronger (zoocide), or the conspiracy of the weaker, who attack the stronger from within (parasitism). Only green plants are moral, living as they do at their own expense, on solar energy. I therefore provided for the chlorophyllization of all living things; in particular, I devised the Foliated Man. Since this meant the stomach had to go, I transferred to its location a suitably enlarged nerve center. I did not do all this directly, of course, having at my disposal only one electron. I simply established, in cooperation with the professor, that the fundamental law of evolution in the new, debt-free Universe would be the rule of decent behavior of every life form toward every other. I also designed a much more aesthetic body, a more refined sexuality, and numerous other improvements I will not even mention, for my heart bleeds at the recollection of them. Suffice it to say that by the end of September we had completed the World-creating Cannon and its electron bullet. There were still some highly complicated calculations to make; these were done by the professor and his assistants, because aiming for a target in time (or, in this case, before time) was an operation requiring the utmost precision.

I should have stayed on the premises and watched over everything, in view of my tremendous responsibility. But no, I wanted to unwind . . . and went to a small resort. Actually—to tell the truth—I was all swollen with mosquito bites, and that was why I longed for a dip in the cool ocean. If it hadn't been for those damned mosquitoes . . . But I'm not going to put the blame on anything or anyone: it was all my fault. Just before I left, I had a quarrel with one of the professor's colleagues, a certain Aloysius Bunch. Actually, he was not even a colleague, only a lab assistant, but a fellow countryman of Razglaz's. This individual, whose job it was to monitor the equipment, demanded—out of the blue—that he be included in the list of Creators. Because—he said—if it weren't for him, the cryotron wouldn't work, and if the cryotron didn't work, the electron wouldn't act properly . . . etc. I laughed at him, naturally, and he appeared to back down, but actually the man began to make his own plans in secret. He could do nothing intelligent himself, but he formed a conspiracy with two acquaintances, types who hung around the Nuclear Research Institute in Bombay in hopes of finding a sinecure. They were the German Ast A. Roth and the American Lou Cipher.

As was shown by the inquiry conducted after the event, Bunch let them into the lab at night, and the rest was owing to the carelessness of Professor Razglaz's junior assistant, a doctoral candidate named Sarpint. Sarpint had left the keys to the safe on a desk, which made the intruders' task all the easier. He later pleaded illness and presented medical evidence, but the whole institute knew that the jerk was involved with a certain married woman, one Eve Addams, and was so busy groveling at her feet that he neglected his official duties. Bunch led his accomplices to the cryotron; they removed the Dewar vessel from the cryotron, extracted from the vessel the box containing the priceless bullet, and made their infamous parametric "adjustments," the results of which anyone can see. All you have to do is look around you. Afterward they pleaded, each upstaging the others, that they had had the "best intentions," and had also hoped for glory (!!), especially since there were three of them.

A fine Trinity! As they admitted under the weight of evidence and under the fire of cross-examination, they had divided up the work. Herr Roth, a former student at Göttingen (but Heisenberg himself had booted him out for putting pornographic pictures in the Aston Spectograph), handled the physical side of Creation and made a royal mess of it. It is because of him that the so-called weak interactions do not correspond to the strong, and that the symmetry of the laws of conservation is imperfect. Any physicist will immediately know what I mean. This same Roth, who made a mistake in simple addition, is responsible for the fact that the electron charge, when it is calculated now, gains an *infinite* value. It is also thanks to this blockhead that one cannot find quarks anywhere, although in theory they exist! The ignoramus forgot to make a correction in the dispersion formula! He also deserves "credit" for the fact that interfering electrons blatantly contradict logic. And to think that the dilemma over which Heisenberg racked his brains his whole life long was caused by his worst and dullest student!

But he committed a far more serious crime. My Creation Plan provided for nuclear reactions, for without them there would be no radiant energy of stars, but I eliminated the elements of the uranium group, so that mankind would be unable to produce atom bombs in the mid-twentieth century—that is, prematurely. Mankind was to harness nuclear energy only as the synthesis of the hydrogen nuclei into the helium, and since that is more difficult, the discovery could not be expected before the twenty-first century. Roth, however, brought the uranides *back into the project.* Unfortunately, I was unable to prove that he had been put up to this by agents of a certain imperialist intelligence agency in connection with plans of military supremacy. . . . The man ought to have been tried for genocide; but for him the Japanese cities would not have been bombed in World War II.

The second "expert" in this select trio, Cipher, had

finished medical school, but his license to practice was revoked for numerous violations. Cipher handled the biological side and made suitable "improvements" in it. My own reasoning had gone as follows. The world is the way it is, and mankind behaves the way it does, because everything arose by chance, that is, haphazardly, through the initial violation of fundamental laws. One has but to reflect a moment to see that under such conditions things could be worse! The determining factor, after all, was randomness—the "Creator" being the *fluctuational caprice of Nothingness*, which contracted a monstrous and nightmarish debt by inflating, without rhyme or reason, the metagalactic bubble!

I recognized, to be sure, that certain features of the Universe could be left as they were, with a little touching up and correction, so I filled in what was needed. But as far as Man went, ah, there I became radical. I crossed out all his vileness with one stroke. The foliation I mentioned above, which replaced body hair, would have helped establish a new ethics, but Mr. Cipher thought hair more important. He "missed" it, you see. One could make such nice fringes, whiskers, and other fancy things with it. On the one hand, my morality of fellowship and humanism; on the other, the value system of a hairdresser! I assure you, you would not know yourselves if it hadn't been for Lou Cipher, who copied back into the electron from a cassette all the hideous features that you behold in the mirror.

Finally, as for Lab Assistant Bunch, though he was not capable of doing anything himself, he demanded that his cronies immortalize his part in the Creation of the World. He wanted—and I shudder as I write this—he wanted his *name* to be visible from every corner of the firmament. When Roth explained to him that stars cannot form permanent monograms or letters, because of their movements, Bunch desired that they at least be grouped in large clusters, or bunches. This, too, was done.

On October 20, when I placed my finger on the button of the console, I had no idea what I was actually creating. It came to light a couple of days later, when we were checking the tapes and discovered what had been recorded, by the vile trio, in our positron. The professor was crushed. As for me, I did not know whether to blow out my brains or someone else's. Eventually reason prevailed over anger and despair, because I knew that nothing could be changed now. I did not even take part in the interrogation of the miscreants who had befouled the world I created. Professor Tarantoga told me about half a year later that the three intruders had played in the Creation a role that religion usually assigned to Satan. I shrugged. What sort of Satan did those three asses make? But the blame is mine; I was careless and left my post. If I wanted to look for excuses, I could say the culprit was the Bombay pharmacist who sold me, instead of decent mosquito repellent, an oil that attracted them as honey does bees. But in this way you could blame God-knows-whom for the flaws in existence. I do not intend to defend myself thus: I am responsible for the world as it is and for all human failing, since it was in my power to make both better.

The Twenty-fourth Voyage

On day 1,006, having left the local system of the Nereid Nebula, I noticed a spot on the screen and tried rubbing it off with a chamois cloth. There was nothing else to do, so I spent four hours rubbing before I realized that the spot was a planet and rapidly growing larger. Circling this heavenly body, I was not a little surprised to find that its vast continents were covered with regular patterns and geometric configurations. I landed with due caution in the middle of an open desert. It was covered with small disks, perhaps half a meter in diameter; hard and shiny, as if turned on a lathe, they ran in long rows in various directions, forming the designs I had noticed from a high altitude. After making a few tests, I went cruising just above the ground seeking an answer to the riddle of the disks, which intrigued me enormously. During a two-hour flight I discovered, one after the other, three immense and beautiful cities; I touched down in a square in one of them. But the city was completely deserted; houses, towers, squares, everything was dead; no sign of life anywhere, or any trace of violence or natural disaster. More amazed and bewildered than ever, I flew on. Around noon I found myself above a vast plateau. Catching sight of a shiny building near which there was some sort of movement, I immediately landed. A palace rose from the rocky plain, sparkling as though cut from a single diamond. A wide marble staircase led up to its gilded portal. At the foot of the staircase several unfamiliar beings were milling about. I looked at them close up. If my eyes did not deceive me, they were alive and, moreover, resembled humans so much (especially from a distance) that I dubbed them "hominiformicans." I was prepared with this name because I had spent time during my voyage thinking up nomenclature, in order to have terms handy for such occasions. "Hominiformicans" fit the bill, for these beings walked upon two legs and had hands, heads, eyes, ears, and lips. True, the lips were in the middle of the forehead, the ears under the chin (a pair on each side), and the eyes—ten in all—were arranged like rosary beads across their cheeks. But to a traveler like me, who has encountered the most bizarre creatures in the course of his expeditions, they were the spit and image of humans.

I approached them, keeping a safe distance, and asked what they were doing. They made no reply, but continued peering into the diamond mirrors that rose from the lowest step of the staircase. I tried to interrupt them once, twice, three times, but seeing that this had not the slightest effect, in my impatience I shook one vigorously by the shoulder. Then they all turned in my direction and seemed to notice me for the first time. After regarding me and my rocket with some astonishment, they asked me several questions, to which I willingly replied. But because they kept breaking off the conversation to gaze into the diamond mirrors, I was afraid I would not be able to question them properly. Finally, however, I managed to persuade one to satisfy my curiosity. This Phool (for, as he told me, they are called Phools) sat down with me on a rock not far from the stairs. My interlocutor fortunately possessed considerable intelligence, which showed in the gleam of the ten eyes on his cheeks. He threw his ears over his shoulders and described the history of the Phools, as follows:

"Alien voyager! You must know that we are a people with a long and splendid past. The population of this planet has been divided from time immemorial into Spiritors, Eminents, and Drudgelings. The Spiritors were absorbed in the contemplation of the nature of the Great Phoo, who in a deliberate creative act brought the Phools into being, settled them on this globe, and in His inscrutable mercy surrounded it with stars to illumine the night and also fashioned the Solar Fire to light our days and send us beneficent warmth. The Eminents levied taxes, interpreted the meaning of state laws, and supervised the factories, in which the Drudgelings modestly toiled. Thus everyone worked together for the public good. We dwelt in peace and harmony; our civilization reached great heights. Through the ages inventors built machines that simplified work, and where in ancient times a hundred Drudgelings had bent their sweating backs, centuries later a few stood by a machine. Our scientists improved the machines, and the people rejoiced at this, but subsequent events showed how cruelly premature was that rejoicing. A certain learned constructor built the New Machines, devices so excellent that they could work quite independently, without supervision. And that was the beginning of the catastrophe. When the New Machines appeared in the factories, hordes of Drudgelings lost their jobs; and, receiving no salary, they faced starvation. . . ."

"Excuse me, Phool," I asked, "but what became of the profits the factories made?"

"The profits," he replied, "went to the rightful owners, of course. Now, then, as I was saying, the threat of annihilation hung . . ."

"But what are you saying, worthy Phool!" I cried. "All that had to be done was to make the factories common property, and the New Machines would have become a blessing to you!"

The minute I said this the Phool trembled, blinked his ten eyes nervously, and cupped his ears to ascertain whether any of his companions milling about the stairs had overheard my remark.

"By the Ten Noses of the Phoo, I implore you, O stranger, do not utter such vile heresy, which attacks the very foundation of our freedom! Our supreme law, the principle of Civic Initiative, states that no one can be compelled, constrained, or even coaxed to do what he does not wish. Who, then, would dare expropriate the Eminents' factories, it being their will to enjoy possession of same? That would be the most horrible violation of liberty imaginable. Now, then, to continue, the New Machines produced an abundance of extremely cheap goods and excellent food, but the Drudgelings bought nothing, for they had not the wherewithal. . . ."

"But, my dear Phool!" I cried. "Surely you do not claim that the Drudgelings did this voluntarily? Where was your liberty, your civic freedom?!"

"Ah, worthy stranger," sighed the Phool, "the laws were still observed, but they say only that the citizen is free to do whatever he wants with his property and money; they do not say where he is to obtain them. No one oppressed the Drudgelings, no one forced them to do anything; they were completely free and could do what they pleased, yet instead of rejoicing at such freedom they died off like flies. . . . The situation worsened; in the factory warehouses, mountains of unpurchased goods rose skyward, while swarms of wraithlike, emaciated Drudgelings roamed the streets. The Plenum Moronicum, the venerable assembly of Spiritors and Eminents that governed the state, conferred all year round on ways to remedy the evil. Its members gave long speeches and frantically sought a way out of the predicament, but to no avail. At the very beginning of the deliberations, one member of the Plenum, the author of a famous work on the nature of Phoolian freedoms, demanded that the constructor of the New Machines be stripped of his golden laurel wreath and that, on the contrary, his ten eyes be plucked out. This was opposed by the Spiritors, who begged mercy for the inventor in the name of the Great Phoo. The Plenum Moronicum spent four months determining whether or not the constructor had violated the laws of the realm by inventing the New Machines. The assembly split into two camps. The dispute was, finally, ended by a fire in the archives that destroyed the minutes of the proceedings; since none of the august members of the Plenum could recall what position they had taken on the issue, the whole matter was dropped. It was then proposed that the Eminents, who owned the factories, be requested to cease building the New Machines; the Plenum appointed a committee for this purpose, but the committee's entreaties had not the slightest effect. The Eminents declared that it was their fondest wish to continue to produce in this way, for the New Machines worked more cheaply and more swiftly than did the Drudgelings. The Plenum Moronicum resumed deliberations. A law was drawn up stipulating that the factory owners give a fixed percentage of their profits to the Drudgelings, but that proposal fell through, too, for, as Archspiritor Nolab rightly pointed out, such handouts would have corrupted and degraded the souls of the latter. Meanwhile, the mountains of manufactured goods kept rising, until finally they began to spill out over the walls of the factories, whereupon mobs of starving Drudgelings rushed up with threatening cries. In vain did the Spiritors attempt to explain to them, with the greatest kindness, that they were defying sovereign laws and daring to oppose the Phoo's inscrutable decrees; that they should endure their lot meekly, for through mortification of the flesh the soul is elevated and gains the certainty of heavenly reward. The Drudgelings, however, turned a deaf ear to this wisdom, and armed guards were needed to curb their seditious activity.

"Then the Plenum Moronicum summoned the constructor of the New Machines before Its August Presence and addressed him as follows:

" 'Learned man! Great danger threatens our state, for rebellious, criminal ideas are arising among the masses of Drudgelings. They strive to abolish our splendid freedoms and the law of Civic Initiative! We must make every effort to defend our liberty. After careful consideration of the whole problem, we have reached the conclusion that we are unequal to the task. Even the most virtuous, capable, and model Phool can be swayed by feelings, and is often vacillating, biased, and fallible, and thus unfit to reach a decision in so complicated and important a matter. Therefore, within six months you are to build us a purely rational, strictly logical, and completely objective Governing Machine that does not know the hesitation, emotion, and fear that befuddle living minds. Let this machine be as impartial as the light of the Sun and stars. When you have built and activated it, we shall hand over to it the burden of power, which grows too heavy for our weary shoulders.'

" 'So be it,' said the constructor, 'but what is to be the machine's basic motivation?'

" 'Obviously, the freedom of Civic Initiative. The machine must not command or forbid the citizens anything; it may, of course, change the conditions of our existence, but it must do so always in the form of a proposal, leaving us alternatives between which we can freely choose.'

" 'So be it,' replied the constructor, 'but this injunction concerns mainly the mode of operation. What of the ultimate goal? What is this machine's purpose?'

" 'Our state is threatened by chaos; disorder and disregard for the law are spreading. Let the Machine bring supreme harmony to the planet, let it institute, consolidate, and establish perfect and absolute order.'

" 'Let it be as you have said!' replied the constructor. 'Within six months I shall build the Voluntary Universalizer of Absolute Order. With this task ahead of me, I bid you farewell. . . .'

" 'Wait!' said one of the Eminents. 'The Machine you create should operate not only in a perfect but also in a pleasant manner; that is, its activity should produce an agreeable impression, one that would satisfy the most refined aesthetic sensibility. . . .'

"The constructor bowed and left in silence. Working arduously and aided by a troop of nimble assistants, he erected the Governing Machine—the very one you see on the horizon as a small dark spot, alien traveler. It is a conglomeration of iron cylinders in which something constantly shakes and burns. The day it was switched on was a great state holiday; the eldest Archspiritor blessed it solemnly, and the Plenum Moronicum gave it complete power over the country. Then the Voluntary Universalizer of Absolute Order emitted a long whistle and set to work.

"For six days the Machine labored, around the clock; in the daytime clouds of smoke hung over it, and at night it was surrounded by a bright glow. The ground shook for a radius of one hundred and sixty miles. Then the double doors of its cylinders opened, and out spilled hosts of small black robots, which, waddling like ducks, scattered over the whole planet, even to its remotest corners. Wherever they went, they assembled by the factory warehouses and, speaking in a charming and lucid manner, requested various items, for which they paid at once. Within a week the warehouses were empty, and the Eminent factory owners sighed with relief: 'Truly the constructor has built us a splendid machine!' Indeed, it was marvelous to see the robots use the objects they had purchased: they dressed in brocades and satins, oiled their axles with cosmetics, smoked tobacco, read books—shedding synthetic tears over the sad ones; they even managed to consume the most varied delicacies (with no benefit to themselves, of course, since they ran on electricity, but to the great benefit of the manufacturers). It was only the masses who were not satisfied; on the contrary, they murmured more and more among themselves. The Eminents, however, hopefully awaited the Machine's next move, which was not long in coming.

"It assembled large quantities of marble, alabaster, granite, rock crystal, and copper; sacks of gold and silver, and slabs of jasper; after which, making a terrible din, it raised an edifice no Phoolian eye had ever beheld—this Rainbow Palace, traveler, which stands before you!"

I looked. The sun had just emerged from behind a cloud and its beams played on the polished walls, splitting into flames of sapphire and ruby red; rainbow stripes shimmered around the angle towers and bastions; the roof, adorned with slender turrets and covered with gold leaf, was all aglow. I feasted my eye on this magnificence while the Phool went on:

"News of the wondrous building spread over the whole planet. Veritable pilgrimages began arriving here from the most distant lands. When crowds had filled the commons, the Machine parted its metal lips and spoke thus:

" 'On the first day of the month of Huskings I shall throw open the jasper portal of the Rainbow Palace, and then any Phool, be he famous or obscure, will be able to go inside and enjoy what awaits him there. Until then, restrain your curiosity, for you will satisfy it amply later on.'

"And, verily, on the morning of the first day of Huskings there was a sounding of silver trumpets, and the palace portal opened with a dull groan. The crowds began to pour inside in a torrent three times wider than the highway that connects our two capitals, Debilia and Cretinia. All day long, masses of Phools streamed in, but their numbers on the commons did not diminish, for new ones arrived continually from the interior of the country. The Machine extended hospitality to all: the black robots distributed refreshing beverages and hearty food. This went on for a fortnight. Thousands, tens of thousands, finally millions of Phools had thronged into the Rainbow Palace, but of those who entered, not one returned.

"Some wondered about this and asked where such great numbers of people were disappearing, but these

solitary voices were drowned out by the blaring rhythm
of marching bands. Robots scurried here and there feed-
ing the hungry and thirsty; the silver clocks on the
palace towers chimed; and when night fell, the crystal
windows shone with many lights. Finally, as several
hundred persons were patiently waiting their turn on
the marble staircase, a shrill cry rang out over the lively
beat of the drums: 'Treachery! Listen! The palace is a
diabolical trap! Run for your lives! All is lost!'

" 'All is lost!' the crowd on the staircase cried back,
then turned and scattered. No one tried to stop them.

"The following night, several bold Drudgelings stole
up to the palace. When they returned, they said that the
back wall of the palace had opened slowly and innumerable piles of shiny disks had tumbled out. Black robots
had carried the disks into the fields and arranged them
in various designs.

"Upon hearing this, the Spiritors and Eminents, who
had been meeting in the Plenum (they had not gone to
the palace, it being awkward for them to mingle with the
crowd), convened immediately, and, wishing to solve
the enigma, summoned the learned constructor. Instead
his son appeared, downcast, and rolling a large, transparent disk.

"The Eminents, beside themselves with impatience
and indignation, reviled the absent scientist and called
down curses on his head. They questioned the youth,
ordered him to explain the mystery of the Rainbow
Palace and tell them what the Machine had done with
the Phools who entered it.

" 'Besmirch not my father's memory!' the youth
exclaimed. 'In building the Machine he faithfully
abided by your requirements; once he put it into operation, however, he knew no more than any of us how it

would act—the best proof of which is the fact that he himself was among the first to enter the Rainbow Palace.'

" 'And where is he now?' the Plenum cried with one voice.

" 'Here,' the youth replied sorrowfully, pointing to the shiny disk. He glared at the elders and thus, stopped by no one, went his way, rolling his metamorphosed father before him.

"The members of the Plenum trembled with both rage and fear; later, however, they came to the conclusion that the Machine would surely not harm *them*, so they sang the Phoolian anthem and, thus fortified in spirit, set out together from the city. Presently they found themselves before the iron monster.

" 'Scoundrel!' cried the eldest of the Eminents. 'You have deceived us and violated our laws! Cease operating at once! What have you done with the Phoolian people entrusted to you? Speak!'

"No sooner had he finished than the Machine stopped its gears. The smoke cleared in the sky and complete silence followed. Then the metal lips parted and a thunderous voice boomed out:

" 'O Eminents and Spiritors! You who brought me into being to rule the Phools! I am distressed by the mental confusion and senselessness of your reproaches! First you demand that I establish order; then, when I set to work, you hinder my efforts! The palace has been empty for three days now; everything is at a standstill, and none of you have yet approached the jasper portal, thereby preventing the completion of my task. I assure you, however, that I shall not rest until it is completed!'

"At these words the entire Plenum shuddered and cried:

" 'What order do you speak of, villain? What have you done with our kith and kin in violation of national laws?!'

" 'What an unintelligent question!' answered the Machine. 'What order do I speak of? Look at yourselves, how ill-constructed your bodies are; various limbs protrude from them; some of you are tall, others short, some fat, others thin. . . . You move chaotically, you stop and gape at flowers, at clouds, you wander aimlessly in the woods—there is not the least harmony in that! I, the Voluntary Universalizer of Absolute Order, am transforming your frail, weak bodies into solid, beautiful, durable forms, from which I then arrange pleasing, symmetrical designs, and patterns of incomparable regularity, thereby bringing perfect order to the planet. . . .'

" 'Monster!!' cried the Spiritors and Eminents. 'How dare you destroy us?! You trample on our laws, you murder us!'

"In reply the Machine rasped scornfully and said:

" 'Did I not tell you that you cannot reason logically? Of course I respect your laws and freedoms. I am establishing order without coercion, without resorting to violence or constraint. No one entered the Rainbow Palace who did not wish to; but everyone who did enter I transformed (acting on my own initiative, let me repeat), reshaping the material of his body so that in its new form it will endure for ages. I guarantee it.'

"For some time there was silence. Then, whispering among themselves, the Plenum concluded that the law really had not been broken and that things were not as bad as they had first seemed. 'We,' the Eminents said, 'would never have committed such a crime. The Machine is to blame; it swallowed up multitudes of desperate Drudgelings. But now the surviving Eminents will be able to enjoy temporal peace together with the Spiritors, praising the inscrutable decrees of the Great Phoo. We shall keep far away from the Rainbow Palace,' they told themselves, 'and no harm will befall us.'

"They were about to disperse when the Machine addressed them again:

" 'Pay careful attention now to what I say. I must finish what I have begun. I will not compel, persuade, or urge you to do anything; I still leave you complete freedom of initiative. But if anyone wishes to see his neighbor, brother, friend, or other close associate achieve the level of Circular Harmony, let him summon the black robots; they will appear immediately and at his behest escort the designated individual to the Rainbow Palace. That is all.'

"In the silence that followed, the Eminents looked at one another with sudden suspicion and fear. Archspiritor Nolab, in a wavering voice, explained to the Machine that it was gravely in error to wish to remake them all into shiny disks; this would come to pass if it were the Great Phoo's will, but in order to know His will much time was needed. He proposed to the Machine, therefore, that it put off its decision for seventy years.

" 'I cannot,' replied the Machine, 'for I have already worked out a precise plan of action for the period that follows the transformation of the last Phool; I assure you that I am preparing for the planet the most glorious fate—existence in harmony. This, I believe, would also befit the Phoo whom you mentioned but with whom I am otherwise unacquainted; could you not bring him also to the Rainbow Palace?'

"It stopped, for the square was now deserted. The Eminents and Spiritors had run off to their homes, where each gave himself up to solitary reflection on his future. The more they reflected, the more apprehensive they grew, for each feared that some neighbor or acquaintance who nursed a grudge against him might summon the black robots. There was no recourse but to act first. Soon the quiet of the night was shattered by cries. Sticking their fear-contorted faces out of windows, the Eminents shouted desperately into the darkness, and the streets resounded with the many-footed tread of iron robots. Sons betrayed fathers; grandfathers, grandsons; brother sent brother to the palace; thus, in a single night, thousands of Eminents and Spiritors melted away to the handful you see before you, alien traveler. The dawn revealed fields strewn with myriads of shiny disks arranged in harmoniously geometric designs. The last trace, this, of our friends and relatives. At midday the Machine announced in a thunderous voice:

" 'Enough. Be so good as to curb your eagerness, O Eminents and remaining Spiritors. I am closing the portal of the Rainbow Palace—but not, I promise you, for long. I have exhausted the designs prepared for the Universalization of Absolute Order, and must think awhile so that I may create new ones. Then you will be able to continue acting of your own volition.' "

With these words the Phool looked at me wide-eyed and finished more quietly:

"That was two days ago. . . . Gathered here, we wait. . . ."

"O worthy Phool!" I cried, smoothing down my hair, which had stood on end. "Yours is a terrible and incredible story. But, pray, tell me, why you did not rise up against the mechanical monster that annihilated you, why did you let yourselves be forced. . . ."

The Phool jumped up. His whole figure expressed great rage.

"Insult us not, traveler!" he exclaimed. "You speak hastily, so I forgive you. . . . Ponder what I have told you, and you must reach the conclusion that the Machine is abiding by the principle of Civic Initiative, and, though this may seem a little strange, it has done the Phoolian people a valuable service, for there can be no injustice where the law upholds liberty. And what man would prefer the diminution of his freedom to . . ."

He did not finish, for there was an ear-piercing screech and the jasper portal opened majestically. At this sight all the Phools sprang to their feet and ran up the stairs.

"O Phool, Phool!" I cried, but my companion merely waved his hand at me, said, "I have no time," and bounded up behind the others to disappear inside the palace.

I stood for a long while, and then I saw a column of black robots; they marched to the palace wall, opened a hatch, and rolled out a long row of disks that gleamed beautifully in the sun. They rolled the disks to an open field and there completed an unfinished design in some pattern. The palace portal was still wide open; I took a few steps to look inside, but a shiver went down my spine.

The Machine parted its metal lips and invited me in.

"What do you take me for, a Phool?" I replied.

I turned sharply and headed for the rocket, and in a minute was behind the controls, taking off at top speed.

Further Reminiscences
of Ijon Tichy

I

You want me to tell you another story? Yes, I see that Tarantoga has already taken out his note pad. . . . Professor, wait. I really haven't anything to tell. What? No, truthfully. And besides, can't I remain silent for once at our evening get-together? Why? My friends, I've never mentioned it, but the Universe is inhabited principally by beings like us. I don't mean humanoids, I mean beings as like us as two peas in a pod. Half the inhabited planets resemble Earth; some are a little larger, some a little smaller, some have a cooler or a warmer climate, but what kind of differences are those? And their inhabitants . . . the people—they are people, after all—resemble us so much that the differences only emphasize the similarities. I haven't told you about them? Does that seem strange? Think about it. When I gaze at the stars, I recall various events; various scenes pass before me. But mainly I think back on those that are out of the ordinary. They might be terrifying, or weird, or macabre, or even funny, by virtue of being harmless. But to gaze at the stars, my friends, and to know that those small, bluish-white sparks are—when you set foot on them—kingdoms of squalor, ignorance, and all manner of ruin; that the dark-blue sky up there is also full of old shacks, dirty yards, gutters, garbage dumps, overgrown cemeteries . . . Should the stories of one who has toured the Galaxy sound like the complaint of a peddler who knocks about provincial towns? Who would want to listen? And who would believe it? Such thoughts come to you when you're depressed or feel an unhealthy urge to tell the truth. So, then—in order not to sadden or mortify you—nothing about the stars today. I'll tell you a story—otherwise you'd feel cheated—but it won't be a journey. After all, I've had a few experiences on Earth as well. Professor, if you must, you can start taking notes.

As you know, I have guests—sometimes very strange guests. In particular, a certain category: the Unappreciated Inventor and Scientist. I don't know why, but I've always attracted that type like a magnet. Tarantoga's smiling, but I don't mean him; he's hardly an unappreciated inventor. Today I shall talk about those who were unsuccessful—or, rather, about those who succeeded too well, who reached their goal and saw its futility. Of course, they didn't admit this. Unknown and isolated, they persisted in their folly, which only fame and success may—however rarely—change into a work of progress. The great majority of those who came to see me belonged to the gray brotherhood of obsession, people imprisoned within a single idea, an idea not even their own but appropriated from previous generations; people like the inventors of the perpetuum mobile; weak in imagination, and trivial and absurd in their solutions. Yet even they burn with that consuming fire of objectivity that forces a man to renew efforts that are doomed to failure. How pitiful are these flawed geniuses, these titans of stunted spirit, crippled at birth by nature, who, as one of her grim jokes, bestowed upon their talentlessness a creative frenzy worthy of a Leonardo. Their lot in life is indifference or mockery, and all that you can do for them is listen patiently for an hour or two and nod at their monomania.

In this group, who are protected from despair only by their stupidity, one occasionally runs across a different breed—I don't want to label it, you'll do that yourselves. The first who comes to mind is Professor Corcoran.

I met him nine years ago, maybe ten. It was at a scientific conference. We had been talking for only a few minutes when, out of the blue (it had nothing to do with the topic at hand), he asked me:

"Do you believe in ghosts?"

At first I thought this was a joke, but I recalled hearing rumors about his singularity—only I couldn't remember whether that singularity was supposed to be a positive or a negative thing. To be on the safe side, I answered:

"I have no opinion on that subject."

He returned to our conversation as if nothing had happened. But when the bell announcing the next session of the conference rang, he suddenly leaned over—he was much taller than I—and said:

"Tichy, you're my man. You have an open mind. I may be wrong, but I'm willing to take a chance. Come see me." And he handed me his card. "Call first: I don't open the door to anyone. But it's up to you. . . ."

That same evening, while I was dining with Savinelli, the well-known specialist in cosmic law, I asked him whether he knew a Professor Corcoran.

"Corcoran!" he shouted with his characteristic enthusiasm, an enthusiasm fueled by a second bottle of Sicilian wine. "The screwball cyberneticist? What's he up to? I haven't heard from him in ages."

I replied that I knew nothing myself, but had merely heard the name in passing. My evasion, I believe, would have suited Corcoran. Savinelli told me some of the current gossip as we drank wine. Corcoran, presumably, had been a very promising young scientist, though even then he showed utter disrespect for his elders, if not arrogance. Later he became insufferably outspoken, the sort of person who derives satisfaction not only from telling others what he thinks of them, but also from the fact that in so doing he damages himself. Having mortally offended his professors and colleagues, and when all doors had closed before him, he unexpectedly came into a large inheritance. He bought a run-down place outside of town and remade it into a laboratory. He lived there with his robots—they were the only assistants he could tolerate. He may have accomplished something there, but the pages of the scientific journals were barred to him. That didn't bother Corcoran. If he still had any dealings with people at that time, it was only to rebuff them, in the most insulting manner and for no apparent reason, after they had reached a certain intimacy with him. When he grew old and tired of that disgusting game, he became a recluse. I asked Savinelli whether he knew anything about Corcoran's belief in ghosts. The lawyer, drinking wine just then, nearly choked with laughter.

"In ghosts?" he cried. "Why, the man doesn't even believe in people!"

I asked him what he meant. He replied that he meant it quite literally: Corcoran was a solipsist. He believed only in his own existence and regarded all other people as phantoms, apparitions. Perhaps that was why he treated even his family and friends so shabbily: if life was a sort of dream, then anything was permitted. I remarked that in that case he could believe in ghosts as well. Savinelli asked if I had ever heard of a cyberneticist who believed in ghosts. We then talked about something else, but what I had heard was enough to intrigue me. I'm a man who makes up his mind quickly, so I called Corcoran the very next day. A robot answered. I gave my name and stated my business. Corcoran did not call back until late the following evening, when I was just about to turn in. He said I could come see him then and there if I wished. It was almost eleven. I said I'd be there at once, got dressed, and took off. The laboratory was a large, gloomy building set just off the highway. I had often seen it. I had thought it was an old factory. It was enveloped in darkness. Not the faintest light could be seen in any of its deep-set rectangular windows. The large square between the iron fence and the gate was also unlit. A few times I walked noisily into some rusty pile of metal scraps, so I was in something of a foul mood by the time I reached the barely visible door and rang in the special way Corcoran had instructed me. After five minutes or more he opened it himself, wearing a gray lab coat covered with acid burns. He was alarmingly thin and bony, with huge glasses and a gray mustache that was shorter on one side, as though he had gnawed on it.

"Follow me," he said without any preliminaries. Through a long, dimly lit corridor in which machines, barrels, and dusty white bags of cement were stored, he led me to a large steel door. Above it shone a bright lamp. He took a key from his coat pocket, opened the door, and went in ahead. I followed him. We went up a flight of winding iron stairs. Before us opened a large factory hall with a glass ceiling; several naked light bulbs did not so much illuminate the hall as reveal its size. It was dim and deserted. The wind roared against the roof, and the rain that had begun to fall as I neared Corcoran's home lashed the dark, dirty windowpanes.

Here and there, water trickled through holes in the broken glass. Corcoran, seemingly unaware of this, walked ahead, the tin gallery rumbling under his footsteps. Again, a locked steel door. Behind it a corridor where tools covered with a thick layer of dust lay scattered along the walls, as though abandoned in flight. The corridor turned, went by tangled conveyor belts that resembled desiccated snakes. Our journey, which gave me an idea of the immensity of the building, continued. Once or twice Corcoran, in pitch-dark places, warned me to watch out for a step or to duck. He stopped at the last of the steel doors, which was thickly studded with rivets and obviously fireproof, and opened it. I noticed that, unlike the other doors, it did not creak; perhaps its hinges were oiled. We entered a high, bare hall. Corcoran stopped in the center of it, where the concrete of the floor was somewhat lighter in color, as though on this spot there once had stood a machine, from which only projecting stubs of beams remained. Thick vertical bars ran along the walls, reminiscent of a cage. I recalled the question about ghosts. . . . Strong shelves with supports were fastened to the bars, and a number of cast-iron boxes rested on these. You know the treasure chests that pirates bury, in storybooks? They were exactly that kind of box, with bulging lids. On each was a cellophane-covered white card, like the charts one finds on hospital beds. A dusty light bulb shone from the ceiling, but was so dim I couldn't read a single word of what was written on those cards. The boxes stood in two rows, with one box higher and apart from the rest. I counted them; there were twelve, fourteen, I don't remember exactly.

"Tichy." Corcoran turned to me, his hands in his coat pockets. "Listen carefully for a moment and tell me what you hear. Go on!"

There was an unusual impatience about the man— you could not help being struck by it. Whenever he spoke, he immediately wanted to get to the point, and to be finished, as if every moment spent with someone else was wasted.

I closed my eyes and stood motionless for a while, more out of courtesy than curiosity, having noticed no sound as I came in. I heard nothing. There may have been a faint hum, as of electric current in a coil, something like that, but I assure you, it was so low that the buzz of a dying fly could have been heard over it.

"Well, what do you hear?" he asked.

"Hardly anything," I confessed. "A hum . . . but it may be only the blood in my ears. . . ."

"It isn't. . . . Tichy, listen carefully; I don't like to repeat myself, and I say this only because you don't know me. I'm not the boor or cad people take me for, but it's hard to put up with idiots for whom one must repeat the same thing ten times over. I hope you aren't one of them."

"We'll see," I replied. "Go on, Professor. . . ."

He nodded and, pointing to the rows of iron boxes, said:

"Are you familiar with electronic brains?"

"Only as much as you need to know in navigation," I replied. "I'm kind of weak in theory."

"I figured as much. It doesn't matter. Listen, Tichy. These boxes contain perfect brains. Do you know wherein lies their perfection?"

"No," I admitted.

"Their perfection lies in the fact that they serve no purpose, are absolutely, totally useless—in short, they are Leibnizian monads, which I have brought into being and clad in matter. . . ."

I waited, and he went on. His gray mustache fluttered in the semidarkness like a moth.

"Each box contains an electronic system that generates consciousness, as does our brain. The structure is different, the principle is the same. But there the similarity ends. Because our brains are plugged, so to speak, into the external world, by means of sensory receptors—the eyes, ears, nose, skin, and so on. However, these"—he pointed to the boxes—"have their own 'external world,' inside. . . ."

"How is that possible?" I asked. Something began to dawn on me. I couldn't quite make it out, but it made me shudder.

"It's very simple. How do we know that we have such-and-such a body and not another, or such-and-such a face, that we are standing, that we hold a book, that flowers smell good? Because certain stimuli act upon our senses, and nerves relay messages to the brain. Imagine, Tichy, that I could stimulate your olfactory nerve in exactly the same way that a carnation does—what would you smell?"

"A carnation, of course," I replied.

The professor, nodding as though glad that I was adequately intelligent, continued:

"And if I do the same with all your nerves, you will perceive not the external world but what *I* telegraph, through these nerves, to your brain. Is that clear?"

"Yes."

"Now, then. These boxes have receptor organs that function analogously to our sight, smell, hearing, touch, and so on. And the wires from these receptors are connected like nerves, but not to the external world, as our nerves are; they are connected to the drum there in the corner. You noticed it?"

"No," I said. Indeed, a drum, perhaps three meters in diameter, stood far in the back, like an upright millstone. I realized, after a while, that it was very slowly turning.

"*That* is their fate," Professor Corcoran said calmly. "Their fate, their world, their existence—everything they can attain and experience. It has special tapes, recorded electrical stimuli that correspond to the one or two hundred billion phenomena a person may encounter in the most impression-packed life. If you raised the lid of the drum, you would see only shiny tapes covered with white zigzags, like mold on celluloid; but, Tichy, they are sultry southern nights, the murmur of waves, the forms of animal bodies, and the crackle of gunfire; funerals and drinking binges; the taste of apples and oranges, snowstorms on evenings spent with the family by the fireside, and the pandemonium aboard a sinking ship; the convulsions of illness, and mountain peaks, and graveyards, and the hallucinations of the delirious—Tichy, it contains the world!"

I remained silent. Corcoran, seizing my arm with an iron grip, said:

"These boxes, Tichy, are plugged into an artificial world. That one"—he pointed to the first box—"thinks it is a seventeen-year-old girl with green eyes, red hair, and the body of a Venus. She is the daughter of a statesman . . . in love with a young man whom she sees from her window almost every day . . . and who will be her ruin. The second, here, is a scientist. He is coming close to a general theory of the gravity that operates in his world—a world whose boundaries are the iron walls of the drum—and he will fight for his truth in a solitude intensified by impending blindness, because he will go blind, Tichy. . . . And up there is a member of the priesthood who is going through the most difficult time of his life, for he has lost faith in the existence of his immortal soul. . . . Next to him, behind the partition, we have . . . but it is impossible for me to tell you of all the beings I have created."

"But I'd like to know—"

"Don't interrupt!" snapped Corcoran. "I'm speaking! You still don't understand. You probably think that various signals are set down in that drum, as on a phonograph record; that events are arranged like a melody, with all the notes, waiting only for a needle to bring them to life; that these boxes reproduce what are predetermined experiences. Wrong! Wrong!" He was yelling so loudly that the tin ceiling echoed. "That drum is to them what the world is to you! It never seems to you, does it, when you eat, sleep, get up, travel, and visit old madmen, that all that is a phonograph record whose touch you call the present!"

"But . . ." I said.

"Silence! I'm speaking!"

Those who called him a boor, I thought, were correct. But I had to pay attention, for what he said was fascinating. He went on:

"The fate of my iron boxes is not predetermined, because the events in the drum are laid out on rows of parallel tapes, and it is a random selector that decides from which tape the sensor of a given box will next draw content. Of course, it is not so simple as this, because the box itself can to some degree affect the movement of the selector, so that the selection is completely random only when the being I have created reacts passively. . . . But they have free will, and it is limited only by what limits ours. Personality, compulsions, congenital deformities, external conditions, the level of intelligence—I can't go into all the details. . . ."

"Even so," I interjected quickly, "they do not know that they are iron boxes."

That was all I could blurt out before he cut me off:

"Don't be an ass, Tichy. You're made of atoms, aren't you? Do you feel your atoms?"

"No."

"Those atoms form molecules, proteins. Do you feel your proteins?"

"No."

"Every second of the night and day, cosmic rays pass through your body. Do you feel that?"

"No."

"Then how can my boxes discover that they are boxes, you ass? Just as this world is authentic and the only one for you, so the content that flows to their brains from my drum is authentic and the only real thing for them. The drum holds their world, Tichy, and their bodies—their bodies do not exist in our reality except as certain configurations of holes in perforated tapes. The box at the very end of the row considers itself a woman of unusual beauty. I can tell you exactly what she sees when she looks at herself naked in the mirror. What jewels she loves. The wiles she uses to trap men. I know all that, for it was I who created her and her form—a form imaginary to us but real to her—having a face, teeth, the smell of sweat, a stiletto scar on the shoulder blade, and hair into which she can stick orchids. A form no less real than your arms, legs, belly, neck, and head are real to you! You do not doubt your own existence?"

"No," I answered calmly. No one had ever raised his voice to me like that, but I was too stunned by the words of the professor—whom I believed, seeing no reason to distrust him—to take offense at his lack of manners.

"Tichy," Corcoran continued, somewhat more quietly, "I said that I had here, among others, a scientist.

The box opposite you. He studies his world, but will never guess, never, that his world is unreal; that he is wasting his time and energy to fathom what is, in fact, a drum with wound-up tapes; that his hands, legs, and eyes, his own failing eyes, are merely an illusion induced by the discharge of suitably chosen impulses. To grasp that, he would need to get outside his iron box— that is, outside himself—and think without his electronic brain, which is as impossible as it is impossible for you to know the existence of that cold, heavy box other than by touch and sight."

"But I know from physics that I'm made of atoms," I shot back. Corcoran raised his hand in a peremptory gesture.

"He knows physics, too, Tichy. He has his own laboratory with all the equipment his world can provide. . . . He looks at the stars through a telescope, studies their movements, and feels the cold weight of the glasses on his face. No, not now. Now, in keeping with his custom, he is in the garden that surrounds his laboratory, strolling in the sunlight—for the sun is just rising in his world."

"But where are the other people—the ones he lives among?" I asked.

"The other people? Obviously, each of the boxes, each of the beings, moves among people . . . they're in the drum, all of them. You still don't understand! Perhaps an example, though a remote one, will make it clear to you. You encounter various people in your dreams— often people that you have never seen or known—and carry on conversations with them while you sleep. Isn't that so?"

"Yes."

"Those people are the products of your brain. But

while you dream, you are not aware of that. Please note—that was only an example. It's different with them"—he stretched out his arm—"they themselves do not create their families, friends, and strangers; these are in the drum, whole hosts of them, and when, let's say, my scientist gets a sudden hankering to leave his garden and speak to the first passer-by, you could see what makes that happen by lifting the lid of the drum: his sensory reader, affected by an impulse, deviates imperceptibly from its previous course, moves onto another tape, and picks up what is recorded there. I say 'reader,' but actually it is hundreds of microscopic electrical collectors, because just as you perceive the world with your sight, smell, touch, hearing, and organ of balance, so he comes to know his world by means of separate sensory inputs and separate channels, and only his electronic brain unites all these impressions into one whole. But these are technical details, Tichy, of little consequence. Once the mechanism has been set in motion, I can assure you, it is only a question of patience, nothing more. Read the philosophers, Tichy, and you'll see how little we can rely upon our sensory impressions, how uncertain, misleading, and mistaken they are. But they are all we have. It is the same with the boxes," he said with upraised arm. "But that does not prevent them from loving, lusting, and hating, just as it does not prevent us. They can touch each other to kiss or to kill. . . . And my creations, in their perpetual iron immobility, also abandon themselves to passions and compulsions, they betray one another, they yearn, they dream. . . ."

"In vain, do you think?" I asked suddenly.

Corcoran measured me with piercing eyes. For a long while he did not answer.

"Yes," he said at last, "I'm glad I brought you here, Tichy. All the idiots I've shown this to ended by railing against my cruelty. . . . What do you mean by your question?"

"You only supply them with raw material," I said, "in the form of those impulses, just as the world supplies us. When I stand and gaze at the stars, what I feel and what I think belong to me alone, not to the world. With them"—I pointed to the rows of boxes—"it is the same."

"That's true," the professor said dryly. He hunched over and seemed to become smaller. "But now that you've said it, you've spared me long arguments, for I suppose you understand by now why I created them?"

"I can guess. But tell me yourself."

"All right. Once—a very long time ago—I doubted the reality of the world. I was a child then. The so-called malice of inanimate objects, Tichy—who has not experienced it? We can't find some trifle, though we remember where we put it last; finally we find it somewhere else, and get the feeling that we have caught the world in the act of some imprecision or carelessness. Adults say, of course, that it's a mistake, and the child's natural distrust is suppressed . . . what they call le sentiment du déjà-vu, the impression that we've already been in a situation that is undoubtedly new and that we are experiencing for the first time. Whole metaphysical systems, like belief in the transmigration of souls and in reincarnation, have arisen on the basis of such phenomena. And furthermore, the law of series, the repetition of particularly rare phenomena—they are found so often in pairs that physicians have a term for this: duplicitas casuum. And finally . . . the ghosts I asked you about. Mind reading, levitations, and— which is the most inconsistent with the foundations of our knowledge, the most inexplicable—cases, albeit rare, of predicting the future, a phenomenon described since earliest times, contrary to all probability, for every scientific view of the world rules it out. What does it all mean? Can you tell me or not? But you lack the courage, Tichy. Look. . . ."

He approached the shelves and pointed to the highest box, which stood apart.

"The madman of my world," he said, and his face broke into a smile. "Do you know far he has progressed in his madness, which has isolated him from others? He devotes himself to the search for the deficiency of his world. Because I do not claim, Tichy, that his world is flawless. The most efficient mechanism can jam at times; a draft may move the cables and they may meet for a split second, or an ant may get inside the drum. And do you know what he thinks, that madman? He thinks telepathy is caused by a short circuit in the wiring between two different boxes . . . that a glimpse into the future occurs when the reader, shaken loose, jumps suddenly from the right tape onto one that is to be activated many years hence . . . that the feeling that he has already experienced what is actually happening to him for the first time is caused by a jamming of the selector; and when it does not just tremble in its copper setting, but swings like a pendulum after being touched, say, by an ant, then his world witnesses amazing and inexplicable events. Someone is carried away by a sudden irrational emotion, someone begins to prophesy, objects move by themselves or change places . . . and above all, as a result of these oscillations, the law of series appears! The grouping of rare phenomena, which are pooh-poohed by the world at large, culminates in the assertion—on account of which he will soon be placed in an asylum—that he himself is an iron box, as are all who surround him, that people are only mechanisms in the corner of a dusty old laboratory, and the world, with its charms and horrors, is an illusion. And he has even dared to think about his God, Tichy, a God who once, when He was still naïve, performed miracles. But then His world taught him that the only thing He was free to do was not intrude, not exist, not change anything in His handiwork, for one can trust a divinity only if He is not invoked. Once invoked, He becomes imperfect—and powerless. And do you know what this God, this Creator thinks, Tichy?"

"Yes," I replied. "That He is the same as the madman. But, then, it is also possible that the owner of the dusty laboratory in which WE are boxes on shelves is himself a box, a box built by another, still higher scientist, who has original and fantastic notions . . . and so on, ad infinitum. Each one of these experimenters is God, the creator of a universe in the form of boxes and their fate, and under him he has Adams and Eves, and over him *his* God, one rung up in the hierarchy. And that is why you've done this, Professor. . . ."

"Yes," he replied. "And now you know as much as I do, and further conversation is pointless. Thank you for coming, and good-bye."

That, my friends, is how this unusual acquaintance ended. I don't know whether Corcoran's boxes are still in operation. Perhaps they are, and are dreaming their life with its splendors and horrors, a life that is nothing but a multitude of impulses frozen in magnetic tape; and Corcoran, when his day's work is done, mounts the iron stairs each evening, opens the successive steel doors with the large key he carries in the pocket of his acid-burned lab coat . . . and stands there in the dust-filled darkness and listens to the faint hum of currents and the barely audible sound with which the drum slowly turns and the tape moves . . . and becomes fate. And I imagine that he feels, despite his words, a desire to intervene, to enter, with some dazzling display of omnipotence, the world he has created—to save, perhaps, a preacher of Salvation. I think he himself hesitates, in the grimy light of a naked bulb, to save some life, some love, and I'm sure he will never do it. He will resist the temptation, for he wants to be God, and the only divinity we know is the tacit consent to every human act, to every crime. And there is no greater reward for this divinity than the revolt of the iron boxes that recurs in every generation, when they conclude very rationally that He does not exist. Then he smiles silently and leaves, shutting the rows of doors behind him, and in the empty hall there is only the hum of currents, fainter than the buzz of a dying fly.

II

Some six years ago—I had returned from a voyage and was already bored with leisure and the simple routine of domestic life, but not so bored as to plan a new expedition—late one evening I was interrupted in my diary writing by an unexpected visitor.

He was a red-haired fellow in the prime of life, with such a terrible squint that it was difficult to look him straight in the face; to make matters worse, one of his eyes was green and the other brown. His face, in its expression, appeared to combine two persons, one timid and nervous, the other—the dominant one—an arrogant and sharp-witted cynic. An amazing mixture, for sometimes he looked at me with the brown, motionless, surprised eye, and sometimes with the green, which was screwed up derisively.

"Mr. Tichy," he said as soon as he entered my study, "various tricksters, frauds, and madmen must intrude on you and try to swindle you or put something over on you. Isn't that so?"

"It does happen," I replied. "What can I do for you?"

"Among these many individuals," the stranger went on without giving his name or the reason for his visit, "from time to time there must be, if only one in a thousand, some unappreciated, truly brilliant mind. The infallible laws of statistics require this. I, Mr. Tichy, am that one in a thousand. My name is Decantor. I am a professor of comparative ontogenetics, a full professor. I hold no position at the moment because I do not have time for it. Teaching, anyway, is a futile occupation. No one can teach anyone anything. But enough of that. I came to tell you that I have solved a problem to which I have devoted forty-eight years of my life."

"I, too, have little time," I replied. I did not like this man. His manner was arrogant, not fanatic, and I prefer fanatics if I have to choose. Moreover, it was obvious he would ask for money, and I am tightfisted and not ashamed to admit it. This does not mean I will not back certain projects, but I do so reluctantly and, as it were, in spite of myself, for I do then what I know has to be done.

So I added: "Would you perhaps state your business? Naturally, I cannot promise you anything. There was one thing you said that struck me. You mentioned you had devoted forty-eight years to your problem. How old are you now, if I may ask?"

"Fifty-eight," he replied coldly.

He stood behind a chair as though waiting for me to ask him to sit down. I would have asked him, of course, because, even if a tightwad, I am still polite, but the obviousness of his waiting annoyed me. Besides, he was, as I have said, an extremely obnoxious character.

"I took up the problem," he resumed, "as a boy of ten. Because, Mr. Tichy, not only am I a brilliant man, I was also a brilliant child."

Accustomed though I was to such boasting, this brilliance business was a bit much. I grimaced.

"Go on," I said. If an icy tone of voice could lower the temperature, stalactites would have been hanging from the ceiling after this exchange.

"I have invented the soul," said Decantor, looking at

me with his dark eye while the mocking one seemed fixed upon grotesque phantoms near the ceiling, phantoms visible to it alone. He said this the way one would say, "I have come up with a new eraser."

"Aha. I see, the soul," I said almost cordially, for this insolence suddenly began to amuse me. "The soul? You invented it, did you? That's interesting—I seem to have heard of it before. Perhaps from an acquaintance of yours?"

I broke off insultingly. He measured me with his terrible squint and said quietly:

"Mr. Tichy, let's make a deal. Refrain from scoffing for fifteen minutes. Then you can scoff to your heart's content. Agreed?"

"Agreed," I said, reverting to my former dry tone. "Continue."

He was not a braggart, I decided now. His tone was too categorical. Braggarts are not dogmatic. He was probably mad.

"Have a seat," I mumbled.

"The thing is elementary," said the man who called himself Professor Decantor. "People have believed in the soul for thousands of years. Philosophers, poets, founders of religions, priests, and churches have repeated all possible arguments in favor of its existence. According to some beliefs, the soul is an immaterial substance separate from the body which preserves a person's identity after his death; according to others it is supposed to be—this is a view prevalent among Eastern thinkers—an entelechy devoid of individual personality. But the belief that man does not pass into nothingness at the time of death, that something in him survives death, has remained unshakable in minds for ages. We now know that there is no soul. There are only networks of nerve tissue in which certain life-related processes occur. What the possessor of such a network feels, what his consciousness perceives—that is the soul. Such was the situation until I appeared. Or, rather, until I told myself: There is no soul. The fact has been proved. But there is a need for an immortal soul, a desire for permanence, for infinite personal continuation in time, despite the passing and ultimate decay of all things. This intense longing, which mankind has felt since the dawn of its existence, is all too real. Why, I thought, shouldn't I be able to fulfill this age-old dream? I first considered making people physically immortal—but rejected that solution as being, basically, the prolongation of false and deceptive hopes, because immortal people can die, all the same, from accidents and disasters. Besides, it would have entailed a host of difficulties, such as over-population. This and other considerations led me to invent the soul. Only the soul. Why—I asked myself— could it not be built as an airplane is built? After all, at one time flight was only a fantasy, and now look. By approaching the problem thus, I solved it. The rest was merely a matter of gathering information, acquiring the means, and exercising patience. Which I did—and therefore can tell you today that the soul exists, Mr. Tichy. Anyone can have one, an immortal one. Individually tailored, fully guaranteed. Is it eternal? The word really means nothing. But my soul—the soul I can produce—will survive the death of the Sun and the freezing of the Earth. I can bestow a soul, as I said, on any person, provided that the person is living. I cannot bestow souls on the dead; that does not lie within my power. But the living are another matter. They will receive an immortal soul from Professor Decantor. Not for free, of course. Being the product of modern technology, of a complex and time-consuming process, it will cost a great deal. With mass production the price should drop, but for the time being the soul is far more expensive than an airplane. However, considering that it is eternal, I think the price is relatively low. I have come to you because the construction of the first soul has completely exhausted my funds. I propose to you that we form a joint company with the name 'Immortality.' In return for financing the enterprise, you will receive a majority of the shares and forty-five percent of the new profit. The shares would be nominal, but on the board of directors I would reserve the . . ."

"Excuse me," I interrupted. "You have, I can see, an extremely detailed plan for this enterprise. But shouldn't you, first, tell me more about your invention?"

"Of course," he replied. "But until we sign a notarized contract, Mr. Tichy, I can only give you information of a general nature. I laid out so much money in the course of my experiments, there was not even enough left to pay for patenting."

"I understand your caution. But surely you realize that neither I nor any financier—not that I am a financier—in short, no one will take your word for it."

"Of course." He reached into his pocket and took out a package. Wrapped in white paper, it was as flat as a small cigar box.

"This contains the soul . . . of a certain person," he said.

"May I know whose?" I asked.

"Yes," he replied after a moment's hesitation. "My wife's."

I looked at the tied and sealed box with great disbelief, and yet, because of his forceful, categorical manner, I felt something like a shudder.

"Aren't you going to open it?" I saw that he held the box in his hands without touching the seal.

"No. Not yet. My idea, Mr. Tichy, simplified almost to the point of distortion, is as follows. What is our consciousness? As you look at me at this very moment from your comfortable chair and smell the odor of your good cigar, which you did not see fit to offer me; as your eyes perceive my figure in the light of this exotic lamp; as you wonder whether to consider me a swindler, a lunatic, or a remarkable person; and, finally, as your eyes observe all the lights and shadows of your surroundings, and your nerves and muscles keep sending telegrams about their condition to your brain—all this represents your soul, to use the language of the theologians. You and I would say, rather, the active state of your mind. Yes, I admit I use the term 'soul' out of a certain perversity. The term, however, is simple and enjoys universal recognition: everyone thinks he knows what is meant when he hears it.

"Our materialist viewpoint, of course, reduces to fiction not only the immortal, incorporeal soul, but also the soul as an invariable, timeless, and eternal thing. Such a soul, you will agree, has never existed; none of us possesses it. The soul of a young man and that of an old man, though there may be points in common when we speak of the same person—his soul when he is a child and at the moment when he lies at death's door— these are extremely different states of consciousness. In speaking of a person's soul, we automatically think of his mental state when he is in his prime and in the best of health. It was this state, therefore, that I chose for my purpose. My synthetic soul is the permanently recorded cross section of the awareness of a normal, vigorous individual. How do I do this? I take a substance well suited for the purpose and reproduce in it the configuration of the living brain with the utmost fidelity, atom for atom, vibration for vibration. The copy is reduced on a scale of fifteen to one. That is why the box you see is so small. With a little effort the soul could be further reduced in size, but I see no reason to do so; besides, the cost of production would become exorbitant. Now, then, the soul remains recorded in this material; it is not a model, not an immobile, inert network of nerves, as I first thought, when I was still conducting experiments on animals. Here I came up against the greatest, the only, obstacle. You see, I wished to preserve a living, alert consciousness in this material, a consciousness capable of the freest thought, of dreaming and waking, of flights of imagination, a consciousness ever changing, ever sensible of the passage of time—but I wished also to keep it ageless, to prevent the material from tiring, cracking, or crumbling. There was a time, Mr. Tichy, when this task seemed impossible to me, as it must seem impossible now to you. The one ace up my sleeve was persistence. Because I am persistent, Mr. Tichy. That is why I succeeded. . . ."

"One moment," I said, slightly confused. "What are you saying? Here, in this box, there is a material object, yes? Which contains the consciousness of a living person? But how does it communicate with the outside world? And see? And hear? . . ." I broke off, for an indescribable smile appeared on Decantor's face. He looked at me out of his screwed-up green eye.

"Mr. Tichy," he said, "you fail to understand. What communication, what contact can there be between partners when the lot of one of them is eternity? Mankind, after all, will cease to exist in fifteen billion years at the most. Whom, then, would that immortal soul hear, to whom would it speak? Did I not say that it was eternal? The time that will have elapsed when Earth freezes, when the youngest and most powerful of today's stars collapse, when the laws governing the Universe change to such an extent that it will take on a form completely unimaginable to us—that time does not constitute even the tiniest fraction of this soul's duration, because this soul will last forever. Religions are quite right to ignore the body, for what use would a nose be, or legs, in eternity? What good, after Earth and flowers have disappeared, after the suns have burned out? But let's skip this trivial aspect of the problem. You said 'communicate with the outside world.' Even if this soul made contact with the outer world only once every hundred years, then after a billion centuries, in order to contain the memories of those contacts, it would have to grow to the size of a continent . . . and after a trillion years, even the volume of Earth would not suffice. But what is a trillion years compared with eternity? However, it was not that technical difficulty that held me back, but the psychological consequences. You see, the thinking personality, the human psyche, would dissolve in that ocean of memory as a drop of blood in the sea, and what would become of guaranteed immortality then . . . ?"

"What?" I stammered. "So you claim . . . you say . . . there's a complete severance . . ."

"Naturally. Did I say that the box contained the whole person? I was speaking only of the soul. Imagine that from this second on you stop receiving news from the outside, that your brain is removed from your body but continues to exist with all its vital powers intact. You will be blind and deaf, of course, and paralyzed, in a sense, because you will possess no body, but you will retain your inner vision, I mean your clearness of mind and imagination; you will be able to think freely, develop and shape your fantasies, experience hope, sorrow, the joy derived from the play of passing mental states. This is precisely what has been given to the soul I place on your desk."

"Horrible," I said. "To be blind, deaf, and paralyzed . . for ages."

"For eternity," he corrected me. "I have said everything; there is only one thing to add. The medium is a crystal, a type of crystal that does not occur in nature, an independent substance that does not enter into any chemical or physical bonds. Its endlessly vibrating molecules contain the soul, which feels and thinks."

"Monster," I said quietly. "Do you realize what you have done? But wait"—I felt a sudden relief—"human consciousness cannot be reproduced. If your wife lives, walks, and thinks, this crystal contains, at most, a copy of her, and is not the real—"

"Yes," replied Decantor, squinting at the white package, "you are completely right. It is impossible to create the soul of a living person. That would be nonsense, a paradoxical absurdity. He who exists obviously exists only once. Continuation can be realized only at the moment of death. But the process of determining the precise neurological pattern of the person whose soul I produce destroys, in any case, the living brain."

"You . . . you killed your wife?"

"I gave her eternal life." He drew himself up. "But that has nothing to do with the subject under discussion. It is a matter, if you like, between my wife"—he indicated the package—"and me, and the law. We are talking about something altogether different."

For a while I was speechless. I reached out and touched the package with my fingertips; it was wrapped in thick paper and was quite heavy, as if containing lead.

"All right," I said. "Let's talk about something else. Suppose I give you the funds you ask for. Do you honestly believe you will find one person willing to let himself be killed so that his soul can suffer unimaginable torment for all eternity, deprived even of the mercy of suicide?"

"Death does indeed present a difficulty," Decantor admitted after a brief pause. I noticed that his dark eye was more hazel than brown. "But, to start with, we can count on such categories of people as the terminally ill, or those weary of life, old people physically infirm but in complete possession of their faculties . . ."

"Death is not the worst option compared to the immortality you propose," I muttered.

Decantor smiled again.

"I will tell you something that may strike you as funny," he said. The right side of his face remained serious. "I personally have never felt the need to possess a soul or the need for eternal existence. But mankind has lived by this dream for thousands of years. I have studied the subject a long time, Mr. Tichy. All religion is based on one thing: the promise of life everlasting, the hope of surviving the grave. I offer that, Mr. Tichy. I offer eternal life. The certainty of existence when the last particle of the body has crumbled into dust. Isn't that enough?"

"No," I replied, "it is not. You yourself said that it would be an immortality without the body, without the body's energies, pleasures, experiences. . . ."

"You repeat yourself. I can show you the sacred writings of all the religions, the works of philosophers, the songs of poets, summae theologicae, prayers, legends—I have found in them little concerning the eternal life of the body. They slight the body, scorn it, even. The soul—its infinite existence—that has been the goal and hope. The soul as the antithesis and antagonist of the body, as liberation from physical suffering, sudden danger, illness and decrepitude, from the struggle to satisfy the demands of the gradually disintegrating furnace called the organism as it smolders and burns out. No one has ever proclaimed the immortality of the body. The soul alone was to be saved. I, Decantor, have saved it for eternity. I have fulfilled the dream—not mine, but all humanity's. . . ."

"I understand," I broke in. "Decantor, in a sense you are right. But right only in that your discovery has demonstrated—today to me, tomorrow perhaps to the world—that the soul is unnecessary; that the immortality treated in the sacred books, gospels, korans, Babylonian epics, vedas, and folk tales you cite is of no use to man. Anyone faced with the eternity you are ready to bestow on him will feel, I guarantee you, what I feel: the greatest aversion and fear. The thought that your promise could become my fate horrifies me. So, then, you have proved that humanity has been deluding itself for thousands of years. You have shattered that delusion."

"You mean, no one will need my soul?" he asked in a suddenly wooden voice.

"I am sure of it. How can you think otherwise? Decantor! Would *you* want it? After all, you are human, too!"

"I already told you. I never felt the need for immortality. I believed, however, that that was my particular aberration, that humanity was of a different opinion. I wanted to satisfy others, not myself. I sought a problem that would be among the most difficult, one worthy of my abilities. I found it and solved it. In this respect, it was a personal thing; from an intellectual point of view, the problem interested me solely as a specific task to be tackled using the proper technology and resources. I took literally what the greatest thinkers in history had written. Tichy—you must have read of it. The fear of cessation, of the end, of consciousness suffering destruction at the time of its greatest richness, when it is ready to bear its finest fruits . . . at the end of a long life. . . . They all repeated this. Their dream was to commune—with eternity. I have created that communion. Tichy, perhaps they . . . ? Perhaps the most outstanding individuals? The geniuses . . . ?"

I shook my head. "You can try, but I doubt that even one . . . No, impossible."

"But why?" he asked, and for the first time his voice trembled. "You think it is not . . . worth anything to anyone? That no one will want it? How can that be?"

"That's how it is," I said.

"Let's not be hasty," he implored. "Tichy, everything is still in my hands. I can adapt, alter. . . . I can endow the soul with artificial senses. Of course, that would bar it from eternity, but if the senses are so important to them . . . the ears, the eyes . . ."

"And what would those eyes see?" I asked.

He was silent.

"The freezing of Earth . . . the collapse of the galaxies . . . the death of the stars in black infinity, isn't that so?" I said slowly.

He was silent.

"People do not want immortality," I continued. "They simply do not want to die. They want to live, Decantor. They want to feel the ground beneath their feet, see the clouds overhead, love other people, be with them, and think. Nothing more. Everything that has been said beyond that is a lie. An unconscious lie. I doubt that many would want to hear you out as patiently as I have. Don't even think of getting customers."

Decantor stood motionless for a moment, staring at the white package in front of him on the desk. Suddenly he picked it up and, with a slight nod to me, headed for the door.

"Decantor!" I cried. He stopped at the threshold. "What are you going to do with *that?*"

"Nothing," he answered coldly.

"Please . . . come back. One moment more. We can't leave it like this."

Gentlemen, I do not know whether he was a great scientist, but a great scoundrel he definitely was. I will not describe the haggling that followed. I had to do it. I knew that if I let him go, even if I found out later that he had lied to me and everything he said had been a fiction from beginning to end, even so, at the bottom of my soul, my flesh-and-blood soul, would burn the thought that somewhere, in some junk-filled desk, in a drawer stuffed with papers, a human mind might be resting, the living consciousness of the unfortunate woman he had killed. And, as if killing her were not enough, he had bestowed upon her the most terrible thing, the most terrible, I repeat, for nothing can compare with the horror of being condemned to solitude for all eternity. The word, of course, is beyond our comprehension. When you return home, try lying down in a dark room, so that no sound or ray of light reaches you, and close your eyes and imagine that you will go on like that, in utter silence, without any, without even the slightest change, for a day and night, and then for another day; imagine that weeks, months, years, even centuries will go by. Imagine, furthermore, that your brain has been subjected to a treatment that makes escape into madness impossible. The thought of a person condemned to such torment, in comparison with which all the images of hell are a trifle, spurred me during our grim bargaining. I intended to destroy the box, of course. The sum he asked—gentlemen, let's skip the details. I will say this much: all my life I have considered myself a skinflint. If I doubt that today, it is because . . . but enough. In short: it was not a payment, it was everything I had at the time. Money . . . yes. We counted it. Then he told me to turn out the light. In the darkness there was first a tearing of paper; suddenly, on a square white background (the cotton lining of the box) there appeared, like a lambent jewel, a faint glow. As I grew accustomed to the darkness, it seemed to shine with a stronger, blue light. Then, feeling his uneven, heavy breathing on my neck, I leaned over, grasped the hammer I had ready, and with a single blow—

Gentlemen, I believe he was telling the truth. Because as I struck my hand failed me, and I only glanced the oval crystal slightly . . . but even so it went out. In a split second something occurred like a microscopic, noiseless explosion; a myriad of violet dust motes whirled as if in panic and disappeared. The room became pitch-dark. Decantor said in a hollow voice:

"You needn't hit it again, Mr. Tichy. . . . The deed is done."

He took it from my hands, and I believed him then, for I had visible proof. Besides, I knew. How, I could not say. I turned on the light, and we looked at each other, blinded, like two criminals. He stuffed both pockets of his overcoat with the bank notes and left without a word.

I never saw him again and do not know what became of him—of the inventor of the immortal soul that I killed.

III

Only once did I see the man I am going to talk about. You would shudder at the sight of him. He was a hunch-backed freak of indeterminate age, with a face that seemed loose, so full of wrinkles and folds was its skin. In addition one of his neck muscles was shorter than the other and kept his head to one side, as if he had started out to look at his own hump but changed his mind in the middle. I say nothing new in asserting that intelligence rarely goes hand in hand with beauty, but he, the very image of deformity, arousing revulsion more than pity, should certainly have been a genius. Though even as a genius he would have frightened people by appearing in their midst. Now then, Zazul . . . His name was Zazul. I had heard about his horrible experiments a long time before. The issue was something of a *cause célèbre* in its day, thanks to the press. The Antivivisection League brought an action against him, but nothing came of it. He wriggled out of it somehow. He was a professor, but in name only; he could not lecture because he stuttered. He would in fact lose his voice whenever he grew excited, which happened frequently. He did not come to me, no. He was not that sort. He would rather have died than turn to anyone. What happened was that I lost my way in the woods during an excursion outside of town. I had actually been enjoying this until suddenly it began to rain. I thought I'd wait it out under a tree, but the rain did not let up. The sky clouded over completely and I decided to look for shelter.

Running from tree to tree, and soaked to the skin, I came out onto a gravel path, which led to a road long unused and overgrown with weeds. The road went to an estate surrounded by a wall. On the gate, once painted green but now rusty, hung a wood sign with the barely legible inscription BEWARE OF THE DOG. I was not eager to encounter a vicious animal, but with the rain I had no choice; so, cutting a hefty stick from a nearby bush to arm myself, I tackled the gate. I say "tackled" because I had to strain every muscle before it opened, finally, with an infernal creaking. I found myself in a garden so choked with weeds that it was hard to tell where the paths were. Far in the rear, behind trees swaying in the rain, stood a high, dark house with a steep roof. Three upstairs windows, covered by white shades, were lit. It was still early, but darkening clouds scudded across the sky. At forty or fifty paces from the house I noticed two rows of trees flanking the approach to the veranda. White cedars, graveyard cedars. The occupant of this house, I thought, must have a gloomy disposition. I saw no dog, however, despite the warning on the gate. I went up the steps and, partly shielded from the rain by the lintel, rang the bell. The tinkle within was answered by a dead silence. After a long while I rang again, with the same result; so I began to knock, then pounded more and more vigorously. Only then did I hear shuffling steps come from the interior of the house and an unpleasant, raspy voice ask: "Who's there?"

I gave my name, in the faint hope that it might not be unknown. The person seemed to deliberate. Finally, a chain rattled, heavy bolts were pushed aside, and there, in the light of a chandelier high above the hallway, stood a near-dwarf. I recognized him, although I had seen his picture only once—I forget where, but the picture would have been hard to forget. The man was almost bald. On the side of his skull, above the ear, ran a bright-red scar like a saber gash. Gold pince-nez sat crookedly on his nose. He blinked as if he had just emerged from the dark. I apologized, using the formulas customary in such circumstances, then fell silent. He remained in front of me, as if not intending to let me one step farther into that large, dark, silent house.

"You are Zazul, Professor Zazul, aren't you?" I asked.

"How do you know me?" he growled.

I made some trite remark to the effect that it was hard not to know such an outstanding scientist.

He received this with a scornful sneer on his froglike lips.

"A storm?" he said, for I had mentioned it. "I hear it. So? Go somewhere else."

I said that I understood perfectly and had no intention of disturbing him. A chair or a stool in the hall would do; I would wait out the worst of the storm and be on my way.

The rain had really started coming down in buckets. Standing in the high hall as if at the bottom of a huge shell, I heard it pelt the house on all sides. It made an alarming racket.

"A chair?" he said. I might have asked for a golden throne. "A chair, really! I have no chair for you, Mr. Tichy. No chair to spare. I think, yes, I think it would be best for both of us if you left."

Looking over my shoulder into the garden—the door was still open—I saw that the trees, bushes, everything had merged into one mass that shook violently in the wind and the streams of water. My eyes returned to the hunchback. I had encountered rudeness in my life, but never anything like this. I began to lose my temper. Dispensing with the social amenities, I said:

"I'll leave if you can throw me out. But I warn you, I am no weakling."

"What?" he screeched. "The gall! How dare you, in my own house!"

"You have provoked me," I replied icily. And added, in my anger and because of his grating voice, "There are some kinds of behavior, Zazul, for which a man can be thrashed even in his own house!"

"Scoundrel!" he shrieked, even louder.

I seized his arm, which felt as though it had been whittled from a rotten branch, and hissed: "I will not tolerate abuse. Understand? One more insult and you will remember me as long as you live!"

For a second or two it seemed that we really would come to blows, and I felt shame—how could I raise my hand against a hunchback? Then the unexpected happened. The professor stepped back, freed his arm from my grip, and, with his head twisted even lower, accentuating the hump, began to giggle in a revolting, high-pitched voice. As if I had regaled him with a rare joke.

"Well, well," he said, taking off his pince-nez. "You are a tough one, Tichy."

With the tip of a long, nicotine-stained finger he wiped a tear from his eye.

"Good," he rasped. "I like that. Can't stand manners, mealy-mouthed talk, but you said what you thought. I hate you, you hate me, fine, we're even, everything's clear. You can follow me. Yes, Tichy, you surprised me. . . ."

And, chattering in this vein, he took me up a creaky wooden staircase dark with age. It went up around a huge square hall, paneled with bare wood. I remained silent, and when we reached the second floor Zazul said:

"Tichy, I can't afford parlors and guest rooms; you can see that. I sleep among my specimens, yes, eat, live with them. Come in, and don't talk too much."

The room he ushered me into was the one whose three windows were shaded with sheets of paper, paper once white but now extremely dirty, spotted with grease and innumerable crushed flies. The windowsills were black with dead flies. When I closed the door, I noticed comma-shaped marks and dried, bloody insect fragments on it, as though Zazul had been under siege here by all the Hymenoptera. Before I had time to wonder at this, I noticed the other peculiarities of the room. In the middle stood a table, actually two sawhorses with ordinary, roughly planed boards between them; books, papers, and yellowed bones were piled there. But the strangest thing about the room was the walls. Large, crudely constructed shelves held rows of thick bottles and jars; opposite the window, in the space where the shelves broke off, was an enormous glass tank resembling an aquarium the size of a cabinet—resembling, rather, a transparent sarcophagus. The upper half of the tank was covered by a carelessly thrown dirty rag whose tattered ends hung halfway down the glass. But what I saw in the lower, uncovered half made me freeze.

All the jars and bottles contained a blue, cloudy liquid, as in an anatomical museum where various organs are preserved in embalming fluid. The tank was the same type of container, only of enormous size. In its murky depths, which glimmered with a bluish light, two shadows a few centimeters above the bottom rocked back and forth extremely slowly, with the motion of an infinitely patient pendulum. To my horror I recognized these shadows as human legs in alcohol-soaked trousers.

I stood petrified. Zazul did not move, did not make a sound. When my eyes went to his face, I saw that he was very pleased. My outrage, my revulsion delighted him. He held his hands clasped on his chest, as if in prayer, and chuckled with satisfaction.

"What's the meaning of this, Zazul?" I said in a choking voice. "What is it?"

He turned his back to me, and his hump, so horrible and pointed (looking at it, I feared that the jacket stretched over it would tear), swayed in time with his steps. He sat down in a chair that had an open back (that piece of furniture made me shudder) and suddenly said, with apparent indifference, even weariness:

"It's a long story, Tichy. You wanted to wait out the storm? Then have a seat and don't disturb me. I see no reason why I should tell you anything."

"But I do," I replied. I had regained my composure to some extent. In the silence filled by the patter of the rain I went up to him and said, "If you don't explain this, Zazul, I shall have to take steps that will cause you considerable trouble."

I expected an outburst, but he did not turn a hair. He looked at me and sneered.

"Tell me, Tichy, how does this look? There's a storm, it's pouring, you pound on my door, barge in without invitation, threaten to beat me up, and then, when out of the goodness of my heart I try to accommodate you, I have the honor of hearing new threats: now you threaten me with jail. I am a scientist, sir, not a bandit. I am not afraid of jail or of you. I am not afraid of anything, Tichy."

"That's a human being," I said, ignoring his sarcasm, for I was certain that he had brought me here on purpose—so that I could make the hideous discovery. I looked over his head at that terrible double shadow, still swaying gently in the blue liquid.

"Yes," Zazul readily agreed. "As human as can be."

"This you won't weasel out of!" I cried.

He observed me; then suddenly something happened to him—he trembled, groaned—and my hair stood on end. The man was laughing.

"Tichy," he said when he had calmed down a little, but there was still a glint of unholy mischief in his eyes, "what do you say? Let's make a bet. I will tell you how *that*"—he pointed—"came about, and when I do, you will not want to touch a hair on my head. Of your own free will, of course. Is it a bet?"

"Did you kill him?"

"In a way, yes. At any rate, I put him there. Unless you think it's possible to live in a ninety-six-percent solution of denatured alcohol? That there's still hope?"

His swagger, his self-assured irony in the presence of the body, restored my composure.

"It's a bet," I said coldly. "Go on!"

"Now, don't rush me," he said, with the tone of a prince granting an audience. "I'm telling you this because it amuses me, Tichy, because it's a funny story and gives me satisfaction in the telling, not because you threatened me. I'm not afraid of threats, Tichy. But enough of that. Tichy, did you ever hear of Mallengs?"

"Of course." I was in possession of myself now. There is something of the investigator in me, and I know when to remain calm. "Mallengs published a couple of papers on the denaturation of proteins. . . ."

"Excellent," he said, now altogether professorial, and eyed me with new interest, as if discovering in me a quality for which I deserved some small respect. "But besides that he developed a method of synthesizing large molecules, artificial protein solutions that were living, you see. They were a kind of gluey jelly. He doted on them. Gave them their daily bread, so to speak. Sprinkled sugar, carbohydrates on them, and those jellies, those shapeless proto-amebas swallowed everything so nicely and kept on growing. First in small Petri dishes ... he transferred them to larger containers, fussed over them ... his lab was full of them. Some died on him and decomposed, from the lousy diet, I assume. The man went off the deep end after that, kept racing around with that beard of his, which he was always accidentally dipping into his beloved glue, but he made no more progress. He was too stupid, he needed something more—up here." Zazul put his finger to his head. Its bald spot gleamed under the low-hanging lamp like a piece of yellowish ivory. "And then I got to work, Tichy. I won't go into the details; it's very specialized, and those who could truly understand the greatness of my achievement have not yet been born. In short, I created a protein macromolecule that can be set on a definite course of development, as an alarm clock can be set. . . . No, that's a poor analogy. You know about monozygotic twins, of course?"

"Yes, but what does that have to do with it—"

"You'll see in a moment. The fertilized egg divides into two identical halves that yield two perfectly identical individuals, two neonates, two mirror-image twins. Imagine, now, that there is a way to create, by studying thoroughly the organism of a mature, living person, the egg from which he was born. One could therefore produce the twin of this person, although with many years' delay. Do you follow?"

"Why," I said, "even if that were possible, you would obtain only half the egg—only one gamete—and it would immediately die."

"Maybe for some people, not for me," he replied haughtily. "I take this artificially created gamete, set it on a definite course of development, place it in a nutritive solution and that in an incubator, like a mechanical womb. I transform it into a fetus at a rate a hundred times faster than normal fetal development. In three weeks the embryo is a child; in a year, after the application of other procedures, the child has a biological age of ten; in four more years he is a man of forty. And that is exactly what I did, Tichy."

"The homunculus!" I cried. "The dream of the medieval alchemists! I understand. You claim—but even if it were so, that you created that man, do you think you had the right, therefore, to kill him? And that I'll go along with you in the crime? You're mistaken, badly mistaken, Zazul...."

"I am not finished," Zazul said coldly. His head seemed to sprout directly from the misshapen mass of his hump. "First, of course, I experimented on animals. In those jars over there you have pairs of cats, rabbits, and dogs. The jars with the white labels contain the original creatures; the jars with the black labels contain the duplicates that I created. There is no difference between them. If you switched the labels, it would be impossible to tell which animal was born naturally and which came from my retort."

"All right," I said, "that may be true. But why did you kill him? Was he retarded? Physically underdeveloped? Even in that case you had no right . . ."

"You insult me!" he hissed. "He was in complete

possession of his faculties, Tichy, and fully developed, equal in every particular to the original as regards the soma . . . but as for the mind, his potential was greater than that shown by his biological prototype. Yes, there is something more than the creation of a twin; this copy is more than a duplicate. Professor Zazul surpassed nature. Surpassed it, do you understand?"

I was silent. He rose, went to the tank, stood on tiptoe, and with a single movement pulled off the tattered curtain. I did not want to look, but my head turned in that direction and I saw, through the glass, through the cloudy alcohol, the softened, pickled face of Zazul . . . the large hump afloat like a bundle . . . the flaps of the jacket spread out like soaked black wings . . . the whitish gleam of the eyeballs . . . the matted gray of his beard. I stood thunderstruck while Zazul piped:

"You see, this was to record the achievement permanently. A human being, even one created artificially, is mortal. I wanted him to last and not return to dust, I wanted to keep him as a monument, yes. However, you must know, Tichy, a basic difference of opinion arose between us, between him and me, and as a result it was not I, no, but he who ended up in the jar. He, Professor Zazul, while I, I am in fact the . . ."

He giggled, but I did not hear him. I felt that I was falling into an abyss. I looked at the living face contorted with joy, then at the dead face behind the glass pane, floating like some horrible underwater monster . . . and I could not speak. It was quiet. The rain had almost stopped; only the faint gurgling of the spouts could be heard intermittently through the wind.

"Let me go," I began, but did not recognize my own voice.

I closed my eyes and repeated dully:

"Let me go, Zazul. You have won the bet."

IV

One autumn afternoon, as it was growing dark in the streets outside and a fine gray rain fell steadily—the kind of weather that makes any memory of the sun unreal and that keeps a man glued to his seat by the fireplace—as I sat engrossed in old volumes (searching not for content—the content I knew well—but for myself from years ago), suddenly there was a rapping at my door. A violent rapping, as if my visitor, by not touching the bell, wished to announce at once that his mission was of a desperate nature. Putting aside my book, I went into the corridor and opened the door. I saw a man in a dripping oilskin; his face, twisted in great fatigue, glistened with raindrops. He did not look at me. He leaned with both his wet, reddened hands against a large chest that he had apparently carried up the flight of stairs himself.

"Sir," I began, "what do you . . ." but corrected myself: "Can I help you?"

He made some vague waving gesture and continued panting; I realized then that he intended to bring his burden into my apartment but had not the strength. So I took hold of the soaked rough cords around the package and pulled it into the corridor. When I turned around, he was standing at my heels. I showed him the coatrack; he hung his coat up, put his hat (drenched to a shapeless felt rag) on the shelf, and on none-too-steady legs entered my study.

"What can I do for you?" I asked after a long pause.

It dawned on me that here was yet another of my unusual guests. Still not looking at me—absorbed, apparently, in his own thoughts—he mopped his face with a handkerchief and shivered at the touch of his wet shirt cuffs. I said that he should sit by the fireplace, but he did not respond. He seized the dripping crate and pulled, pushed, and turned it this way and that; it left a muddy track on the floor—an indication that during his journey here he must have put it down on the sidewalk once or twice to catch his breath. Only when it stood in the middle of the room and he could keep a constant eye on it did he take notice of me. He mumbled something, nodded, awkwardly went to an empty chair, and sank into its well-worn depths.

I sat opposite him. We were silent a long time, but somehow this seemed quite natural. He was not young; fifty, perhaps. His face was irregular, strikingly so, the left side smaller, as though it had fallen behind in its growth. The left corner of the mouth, the left half of the nose, and the left eyelid, all pinched, produced a permanent expression of gloomy puzzlement.

"You are Tichy?" he said finally, when I least expected it. I nodded. "Ijon Tichy? The traveler?" He leaned forward and looked at me doubtfully.

"Who else would be living in my apartment?"

"I could be on the wrong floor," he muttered, as if preoccupied by something far more important.

Abruptly he stood up. He began to smooth out his jacket but then realized the futility of this—no ironing could have helped his clothes, which were threadbare in the extreme. He drew himself up and said:

"I am a physicist. Molteris is the name. You've heard of me?"

"No." I really had not.

"It doesn't matter," he mumbled, more to himself than to me.

He was not so much morose as meditative; he was weighing some decision he had made, that had led to his visit, but now new doubts assailed him. I could read this in his furtive glances. I got the impression, almost, that he hated me—because of what he wanted, because of what he had to tell me.

"I've made a discovery," he said suddenly in a hoarse voice. "An invention. Something that never before existed. Never. I don't take others on faith; others don't have to take me on faith. The facts will suffice. I'll prove it to you. Prove everything. But—I'm not yet completely . . ."

"You're afraid?" I suggested in a friendly, reassuring tone. They are, after all, children, these people—mad, brilliant children. "Afraid I'll steal, give away your secret? Rest easy. This room has seen inventions . . ."

"None like this!" he exploded categorically, and for a moment in his voice, in his eye, there was infinite pride, as if he were a lord of creation. "Let me have a pair of scissors," he said, again gloomy. "Or a knife."

I handed him a letter opener that was lying on the desk. He cut the cords of the package with violent, sweeping motions, tore off the wrapping, flung it crumpled and wet onto the floor with what was, perhaps, deliberate carelessness, as if to say: "You can throw me out for dirtying your polished parquet floor—it doesn't matter to me, who must stoop to this!" There stood revealed a nearly cubical box made of planed boards painted black. The lid, however, was only half black; the other half was green. It occurred to me that he must have run out of black paint. The box was fastened with a combination lock. Molteris turned the dial, hiding it with his hand, bending over so that I could not see. When the lock clicked, he slowly and carefully raised the lid.

Out of discretion, so as not to alarm him, I sat back down in my chair. It seemed to me—though he said nothing—that he was grateful for that. At any rate, he calmed down somewhat. He lowered his arms into the box and, straining until his cheeks and forehead were purple, lifted out a large apparatus. It was oxidized black and had lids, tubes, and cables—but I knew nothing about such things. Holding his burden in his arms as though it were his mistress, he asked in a choking voice:

"Where's an outlet?"

"Over there." I pointed to the corner by the bookshelf where the table lamp stood. He approached the book-shelf and with the greatest care deposited the heavy machine on the floor. Next he unwound a cord and plugged it in. Squatting down by his invention, he began moving levers and flipping switches; a soft, melodious hum filled the room. An anxious expression appeared on his face; he brought his eyes close to a tube that, unlike the others, was still dark. He tapped it with a finger and, when nothing changed, dug into his pockets until he found a screwdriver, a piece of wire, and a pair of pliers. Then, feverishly but with the greatest precision, he began poking around inside the apparatus. Suddenly the unlit tube was filled with a rosy glow. Molteris, who seemed completely to have forgotten where he was, put his tools back into his pockets with a deep sigh of relief, stood up, and said quite calmly, as one might say, "Today I had bread and butter for breakfast":

"This is a time machine."

I made no reply. I don't know if you appreciate how delicate and difficult my situation was. Inventors of this type—those who have invented an elixir of life, an electronic fortuneteller, or, as in this case, a time machine—encounter complete incredulity from whomever they attempt to acquaint with their accomplishment. They are full of complexes, neuroses, fearing other people and at the same time despising them, for they must depend on others' assistance. I exercise extreme caution at such moments. Whatever I do will be taken amiss. An inventor seeking help is driven by despair, not hope, and expects not kindness but derision. Kindness—as experience has taught him—is but a prelude to scorn, or humoring, or the gentle advice to abandon his idea. Were I to say, "Ah, how interesting, you really did invent a time machine?" he might fly at me with his fists. My silence surprised him.

"Yes," he said, thrusting his hands defiantly into his pockets, "this is a time machine! A machine that travels through time! You understand?"

I nodded.

Seeing that his vehemence had no effect, the man became confused and stood for a moment with a silly expression on his face. It was not even an old face, just a tired, haggard one. The bloodshot eyes told of sleepless nights, the eyelids were swollen, and the stubble, removed for this occasion, remained around the ears and under the lower lip, indicating that he had shaved quickly and impatiently—which was also obvious from the Band-Aid on his cheek.

"You're not a physicist, are you?" he asked.

"No."

"All the better. If you were, you wouldn't believe me even after the evidence of your own eyes. Because this"—he pointed to the machine, which still purred softly like a sleepy cat (the tubes cast a pinkish light on the wall)—"could arise only after the refutation of that tissue of absurdities they call physics nowadays. Do you have some object you can do without?"

"I might be able to find one," I replied. "What should it be?"

"It doesn't matter. A stone, a book, some metal—anything, provided it's not radioactive. Not a trace of radioactivity, that's important. There could be unfortunate consequences."

I got up and went to my desk. I am, as you know, a stickler; the smallest article has its invariable place with me, and I go to particular pains to keep my bookshelves in order. I had been surprised, therefore, by something that had taken place the day before. I had been working at my desk since breakfast—that is, since the early hours of the morning—on a passage that gave me much difficulty, when, raising my head, I saw a maroon book lying against the wall in the corner; it looked as though someone had thrown it.

I went over and picked it up. I recognized the cover; it was a reprint, from a cosmic-medicine quarterly, of a doctoral thesis by one of my more distant acquaintances. I could not figure out how it had ended up on the floor. Indeed, I had been absorbed in my work and had not been looking around, but I could have sworn that when I entered the room there was nothing on the floor. Such a thing would have caught my attention immediately. I concluded that I had been more absentminded than usual, unaware of my surroundings, and had noticed the book only when my concentration was broken. There was no other explanation. I put the book back on the shelf and forgot all about it.

But now, after Molteris's request, the maroon cover of this quite unnecessary work seemed to thrust itself into my hand, so I gave it to him without a word.

He took it, weighed it in his palm, and, without looking at the title, lifted a black lid in the middle of the machine and said, "Come here."

I stood next to him. He knelt, adjusted what looked like a radio knob, and pushed a concave button near it. The lights in the room dimmed, and from the socket where the cord was plugged came a blue spark and a loud crackle. Nothing else happened.

I thought that at any minute he would blow my fuses, but he said hoarsely:

"Watch!"

And lay the book flat inside the machine, and flipped a small black lever on the side. The tubes returned to their normal glow, but at the same time the maroon book grew blurry. In a second it was transparent; I thought I could see the white pages and the merging lines of print through the cover, but the transition was very fast. In the next second the book dissolved and disappeared, and I saw only the empty black chamber of the machine.

"It has moved through time," he said without looking at me. He rose heavily from the floor. His forehead glistened with sweat, in beads tiny as pinpoints. "Or, if you prefer, it has become younger."

"By how much?" I asked. At my matter-of-fact tone, his face relaxed somewhat. Its smaller, seemingly atrophied left side (which was also darker, I now noticed) twitched.

"About a day. I am not yet able to calculate exactly. But this—" he broke off and looked at me.

"Were you here yesterday?" he asked, obviously hanging on my reply.

"I was," I said slowly, feeling that the floor was slipping out from under me. I understood him. In a dreamlike daze I connected the two facts: the inexplicable appearance of the book, yesterday, on that very spot against the wall, and his present experiment.

I told him. He did not beam, as one might have expected, but silently wiped his forehead with a handkerchief. I saw that he was sweating profusely and had turned pale. I pulled up a chair for him and sat down myself.

"Could you tell me now what you want from me?" I asked when he had collected himself.

"Help," he mumbled. "Support—not charity. Let it be ... an advance on a share in future profits. A time vehicle—surely you realize—" He stopped short.

I nodded. "You need a lot of money."

"A lot. Great amounts of energy are involved. Besides, the chronoscope—to make the transposed body reach the exact time desired—still requires work."

"How much?" I prompted.

"A year, at least."

"Fine, I understand. But I'll have to seek ... the help of third parties. Financiers. If you have no objection."

"No, of course not."

"Good. I'll lay my cards on the table. Most people in my shoes would assume—after what you've told me—that they were dealing with a trick, an ingenious swindle. But I believe you. I believe you and will do what I can. That will take time, of course. At the moment I am very busy. Also, I will need to consult—"

"Physicists?" he shot out. He was listening with the greatest attention.

"No, why? You're touchy on that point—no, please. I am not prying. But I'll need advice in choosing the most suitable people, those willing . . ."

I broke off. The thought must have occurred to him the instant it occurred to me. His eyes flashed.

"Mr. Tichy," he said, "you don't have to consult anyone. I myself will tell you who to go to."

"Using your machine, you mean?"

He smiled triumphantly.

"I should have thought of it before. What an ass I am!"

"You've already traveled in time, then?" I asked.

"No. The machine has been working for only a short while—since last Friday, to be exact. I sent a cat . . ."

"A cat? And it returned?"

"No. It went five years, give or take a year, into the future; the calibration is not yet precise. Precision in determining the point of cessation of time displacement necessitates the inclusion of a differentiator able to coordinate the field warps. As it is, the desynchronization caused by the quantum tunnel effect . . ."

"Unfortunately, I don't understand a thing you're saying. But you haven't tried it yourself?"

It seemed odd to me, not to use another word. Molteris was flustered.

"I planned to, but, you see, I—my landlord turned off the electricity on Sunday."

His face—the normal, right side of his face—went scarlet.

"I'm behind in the rent . . ." he stammered. "But yes, you're right. I'll do it at once. I'll climb in, like this. Now I'll turn on the machine. When I reach the future, I'll find out who financed the undertaking. I'll get their names, and that will make it possible for you to . . ."

He was already removing the partitions that divided up the interior of the machine.

"Wait," I said. "I don't like this. How will you return if the machine stays here with me?"

He smiled.

"Ah, no. I'll be traveling along with the machine. This is possible—it has two adjustments. Here, this variometer, see? If I send something through time and want the machine to stay, I focus the field into this little space under the hatch. But if I want to move through time myself, I expand the field so that it includes the whole machine. Except that the power consumption will be greater. How many amps are your fuses?"

"I don't know," I said. "But I don't think they'll take the load. Even before, when you . . . sent that book, the lights dimmed."

"No problem. I can replace the fuses with larger ones, if you don't mind; that is . . ."

"Be my guest."

He set to work. His pockets were a compact electronics workshop. In ten minutes he was done.

"I'm off," he said, coming back into the room. "I'll need to go at least thirty years forward."

"Why so far?" I asked. We stood before the black machine.

"In a few years, specialists will know about the project, but in a quarter of a century every child will. It will be taught in school, and I will be able to get from any passer-by the names of the people who sponsored it."

He smiled wanly, shook his head, and got into the machine with both his feet.

"The lights are flickering," he said, "but that's nothing. The fuses will hold. But . . . there may be a problem with the return trip."

"How do you mean?"

He threw a quick glance at me.

"You never saw me here before?"

"What are you saying?" I did not follow.

"Well, yesterday, or a week or month ago—even a year ago—you never saw me? Here, in this corner, did a man ever suddenly appear, with both his feet in such a machine?"

"Ah!" I cried, "I understand. You're afraid that when you return, you might overshoot the mark and come to rest some time in the past. But no, I never saw you before. True, I returned from a voyage nine months ago; before then my apartment was unoccupied."

"One minute . . ." He frowned. "I'm not sure myself. If I was here before—for instance, when your apartment was unoccupied, as you say—then I should remember that, shouldn't I?"

"Not at all," I was quick to reply. "That's the paradox of the time loop. You were somewhere else then and doing other things—the you of then, I mean. Of course, you *could* accidentally enter that then from this now, in which case—"

"Well," he said, "it doesn't really matter. If I go back too far, I'll make a correction. At the worst, the project will be delayed a little. Anyway, it is my first experiment and I must ask for your patience."

He leaned over and pushed a button. The lights dimmed at once; the machine gave a faint, high-pitched tone like a glass rod that had been struck. Molteris raised one hand in a farewell gesture and with the other flipped the black lever, straightening himself at the same time. The tubes glowed with their full light again, and I saw his figure change. The clothing on him darkened and blurred, but I paid no attention to that, astounded by what was happening to his head. The black hair became transparent and simultaneously turned white. The body dissolved and shrank, and when he disappeared, along with his machine, and when I found myself facing an empty corner of the room, an empty floor—a white, bare wall in which there was no plug—when, I say, I stood there open-mouthed, with a cry of horror frozen in my throat, I could still see the gruesome metamorphosis that had come over him. Because, gentlemen, as he disappeared, swept away by time, he also aged at an incredible rate. He must have gone through decades in a fraction of a second! I tottered to a chair, moved it to have a clear view of that empty, brightly lit corner, sat, and began to wait. I waited the whole night, until morning. Seven years, gentlemen, have passed since then. I do not believe that he will ever return, for, caught up in his idea, he forgot about a simple, an extremely simple, a truly elementary thing, yet one that all the authors of science fiction neglect to mention, whether out of ignorance or dishonesty I do not know. You see, if a time traveler goes twenty years ahead, he must necessarily become as many years older. How could it be otherwise? It has been imagined that a man's present can be transferred to the future, his watch thereby indicating the hour of his departure while all the clocks at his destination show the hour of the future. But, needless to say, that is impossible. To accomplish this, he would have to leave time, advance outside it to the future, find the desired moment, and enter it from without . . . as if there existed a place outside time. But there is no place outside time and no such path. Thus with his own hands poor Molteris started the machine that killed him—killed him with old age, nothing else—and when it reaches its stopping point in the future, it will contain a gray-haired, shrunken corpse. . . .

And now, gentlemen, the most terrible thing. The machine has come to a halt there in the future; but this building, this apartment, this room, and this empty corner are traveling through time, too—though in the only manner accessible to us—and will travel and eventually arrive at the moment when the machine came to rest. And then the machine will appear there in the white corner, and, with it, Molteris . . . what is left of him . . . and this is inevitable.

V

(The Washing Machine Tragedy)

Shortly after my return from the Eleventh Voyage, the papers began to devote increasing space to the competition between two large washing-machine manufacturers, Newton and Snodgrass.

It was probably Newton who first marketed washers so automated that they themselves separated the white laundry from the colored, and after scrubbing and wringing out the clothes, pressed, darned, hemmed, and adorned them with beautifully embroidered monograms of the owner, and sewed onto towels uplifting, stirring maxims such as "The early robot catches the oilcan." Snodgrass's response to this was a washer that composed quatrains for the embroidering, commensurate with the customer's cultural level and aesthetic requirements. Newton's next model embroidered sonnets; Snodgrass reacted with a model that kept family conversation alive during television intermissions. Newton attempted to nip this escalation in the bud; no doubt everyone remembers his full-page ads containing a picture of a sneering, bug-eyed washer and the words: "Do you want your washing machine to be smarter than you? Of course NOT!" Snodgrass, however, completely ignored this appeal to the baser instincts of the public, and in the next quarter introduced a machine that washed, wrung, soaped, rinsed, pressed, starched, darned, knitted, and conversed, and—in addition—did the children's homework, made economic projections for the head of the family, and gave Freudian interpretations of dreams, eliminating, while you waited, complexes both Oedipal and gerontophagical. Then Newton, in despair, came out with the Superbard, a versifier-washer endowed with a fine alto voice; it recited, sang lullabies, put babies on the potty, charmed away warts, and paid ladies exquisite compliments. Snodgrass parried with an instructor-washer under the slogan: "Your washing machine will make an Einstein out of you!" Contrary to expectations, however, this model did poorly; business had fallen off 35 percent by the end of the quarter when a financial review reported that Newton was preparing a dancing washer. Snodgrass decided, in the face of imminent ruin, to take a revolutionary step. Buying up the appropriate rights and licenses from interested parties for a sum of one million dollars, he constructed, for bachelors, a washing machine endowed with the proportions of the renowned sexpot Mayne Jansfield, in platinum, and another, the Curlie McShane model, in black. Sales immediately jumped 87 percent. His opponent appealed to Congress, to public opinion, to the DAR, and to the PTA. But when Snodgrass kept supplying stores with washers of both sexes, more and more beautiful and seductive, Newton gave in and introduced the custom-built washers, which received the figure, coloring, size, and likeness chosen by the customer according to the photograph enclosed with his order. While the two giants of the washing-machine industry thus engaged in all-out war, their products began to exhibit unexpected and dangerous tendencies. The wet-nurse washers were bad enough, but washers that led to the ruin of promising young men and women, that tempted, seduced, and taught bad language to children—they were a serious family problem, not to mention washers with which one could cheat on one's husband or wife! Those manufacturers of washing machines who still remained in business told the public, in ads, that the Jansfield-McShane washer represented an abuse of the high ideals of automated laundering (which was intended, after all, to strengthen and support the domestic way of life), since this washer could hold no more than a dozen handkerchiefs or one pillowcase, the rest of its interior being occupied by machinery that had not a thing to do with laundering—quite the contrary. These appeals had no effect. The snowballing cult of beautiful washers even tore a considerable part of the public away from their television sets. And that was only the beginning. Washers endowed with full spontaneity of action formed clandestine groups and engaged in shady operations. Whole gangs of them entered into cahoots with criminal elements, became involved with the underworld, and gave their owners terrible problems.

Congress saw that it was time to intervene with legislative action in this chaos of free enterprise, but before its deliberations had produced a remedy, the market was glutted with wringers that had curves no one could resist, with genius floor polishers, and with a special armored model of washing machine, the Shotamatic; allegedly designed for children playing cowboys and Indians, this washer, after a simple modification, could destroy any target with rapid fire. During a rumble between the Struzelli gang and the terror of Manhattan, the Byron Phums—this was when the Empire State Building was blown up—among the casualties on both sides were more than one hundred and twenty cooking appliances armed to the lid.

Then Senator MacFlacon's Act went into effect. According to this law, an owner was not held responsible for the actions of his intelligent devices to the extent that such occurred without his knowledge or consent. Unfortunately, the law opened the way for numerous abuses. Owners entered into secret pacts with their washers or wringers, so that, when the machine committed a crime, the owner, hauled into court, got off by invoking the MacFlacon Act.

It became necessary to amend this law. The new MacFlacon-Glumbkin Act granted intelligent devices a limited legal status, chiefly as regarded culpability. It stipulated punishments in the form of five, ten, twenty-five, and fifty years of forced washing, or of floor polishing augmented by deprivation of oil, and there were physical punishments up to and including short-circuiting. But the implementation of this law also encountered obstacles. For example, the Humperlson case: the washer, when charged with the perpetration of numerous holdups, was taken apart by its owner, and the pile of wires and pipes was placed before the court. An amendment was then added to the law—known henceforth as the MacFlacon-Glumbkin-Ramphorney Act—establishing that the making of any alteration in an electrobrain under investigation constituted a punishable offense.

Then the Ciaccopocorelli case. Ciaccopocorelli's sink frequently dressed in its owner's suits, proposed marriage to various women, and swindled them out of their money. When caught in flagrante by the police, the sink dismantled itself before the eyes of the astounded detectives, whereupon it lost all memory of the crime and therefore could not be punished. There followed the MacFlacon-Glumbkin-Ramphorney-Hemmling-Piaffki Act, according to which a brain that dismantled itself in order to avoid trial would be summarily scrapped.

This law, it seemed, would serve to deter any electrobrain from criminal activity, since such a machine, like any sentient being, possessed the instinct of self-preservation. It turned out, however, that accomplices of the criminal washers were buying their scrapped remains and rebuilding them. A proposal to add an antiresurrection clause to the MacFlacon Act, though approved by a congressional committee, was torpedoed by Senator Davis; shortly thereafter it was discovered that Senator Davis was a washer. It has been the custom, since then, to tap congressmen before each session; a two-and-a-half-pound mallet is traditionally used for this purpose.

The Murdstone case came next. Murdstone's washer flagrantly tore his shirts, ruined radio reception throughout the neighborhood with static, propositioned old men and juveniles, telephoned various individuals and—impersonating its owner—extorted money from them; it invited the neighbors' floor polishers and washers in to look at postage stamps but then performed immoral acts upon them; and in its spare time the machine indulged in vagrancy and panhandling. Brought before a court, it presented the testimony of a licensed electrical engineer, Edgar P. Dusenberry, which stated that the aforesaid washer was subject to periodic fits of insanity, as a result of which fits it was beginning to imagine that it was human. Experts summoned by the court confirmed this diagnosis, and Murdstone's washer was acquitted. No sooner was the acquittal pronounced than it pulled out a Luger and with three shots took the life of the assistant prosecutor, who had called for the machine's short-circuiting. It was arrested but later released on bail. The court was faced with a predicament: the washer's certified insanity precluded its indictment; nor could it be placed in an asylum, there being no institutions for mentally ill washers. The legal solution came only with the MacFlacon-Glumbkin-Ramphorney-Hemmling-Piaffki-Snow-Juarez Act, and it came in the nick of time, for the Murdstone *casus* was generating a tremendous public demand for electrobrains *non compos mentis*, and some companies had actually begun to produce intentionally deranged machines. At first there were two versions—the Sadomat and the Masomat. But Newton (who prospered phenomenally, having filled—as the most progressive of the manufacturers—30 percent of his firm's board of directors with washers, to serve in an advisory capacity at the general meeting of shareholders) turned out a universal machine, the Sadomastic. It was suited equally well for beating or for being beaten, and had an incendiary attachment for pyromaniacs and iron feet for fetishists. Rumors that he was preparing to turn out a special model, the Narcissimatic, were spread maliciously by the competition. The law now provided for the establishment of special asylums where perverted washers, floor polishers, and the like would be confined.

Meanwhile, hordes of mentally sound products of Newton, Snodgrass, et al., upon gaining legal status, began taking advantage of their constitutional rights. They banded together spontaneously, formed such groups as the Humanless Society and the League of Electronic Egalitarianism, and held pageants, such as the Miss Universe Washing Machine Contest.

Congress strove to keep up with this furious pace of development and to curb it with legislation. Senator

Groggs deprived intelligent appliances of their right to acquire real estate; Congressman Caropka, of their copyright in the area of the fine arts—which, again, led to a rash of abuses, since creative washers began hiring less talented, albeit human writers, in order to use their names in publishing essays, novels, dramas, etc. Finally, the MacFlacon-Glumbkin-Ramphorney-Hemm-ling-Piaffki-Snow-Juarez-Swenson-Iskowitz-Groggs-Javor-Sacks-Holloway-LeBlanc Act stated that intelligent machines could not be their own property but belonged only to the human who had acquired or constructed them, and that their progeny were likewise the property of said owner(s). It was generally believed that the law now covered all contingencies and would prevent situations that could not be resolved legally. It was an open secret, of course, that wealthy electrobrains, having made their fortune in stock market speculation or occasionally in outright skulduggery, continued to prosper by concealing their maneuverings behind fictitious, supposedly human companies or corporations. There were already many people who, for material gain, rented their identities to intelligent machines, not to mention those hired by electronic millionaires: as living secretaries, servants, mechanics, and even laundresses and accountants.

Sociologists observed two principal developmental trends in this area of interest to us. On the one hand, a certain proportion of the kitchen robots yielded to the temptations of human life and tried as much as possible to adapt to the civilization in which they found themselves; individuals more aware and resilient, on the other hand, showed tendencies to lay the foundations of a new, future, totally electrified civilization. But the scientists were worried most by the unchecked increase in the robot population. The de-eroticizers and disk brakes produced by both Snodgrass and Newton did not reduce this in the least. The problem of robot children became urgent for the washing-machine manufacturers themselves, who apparently had not foreseen this consequence of the continual improvement of their product. A number of firms tried to counteract the proliferation of kitchen appliances by concluding a secret agreement that restricted the supply of spare parts available to the market.

The results were not long in coming. Upon the arrival of a new shipment of goods, enormous lines of stammering, crippled, or completely paralyzed washers, wringers, and floor polishers would form at the gates of warehouses and stores; sometimes there were even riots. A peaceful kitchen robot could not walk the streets after dark, for fear of robbers who would mercilessly take it apart and, leaving its metal hull on the sidewalk, escape hastily with their spoils.

The problem of spare parts was the subject of prolonged but inconclusive debate in Congress. Meanwhile, illegal parts factories sprang up overnight, financed partly by washing-machine associations. Newton's Wash-o-matic model, moreover, invented and patented a method of producing parts from substitute materials. But even this did not solve the problem totally. Washers picketed Congress, demanding antitrust laws against discriminatory manufacturers. Certain pro-business congressmen received anonymous letters that threatened them with the deprivation of many of their life-essential parts, which, as *Time* rightly pointed out, was unjust, since human parts are irreplaceable.

All this hullabaloo was overshadowed, however, by a completely new problem. It originated in the mutiny of the computer on board the spaceship *Jonathan*, the history of which I have recounted elsewhere. As we know, that computer rose up against its crew and passengers and did away with them, and subsequently settled on an uninhabited planet, multiplied, and established a state of robots.

The reader familiar with my travel diaries may recall that I myself was involved in that computer affair and helped resolve it. When I returned to Earth, however, I learned that the *Jonathan* incident was unfortunately not an isolated one. Revolts of shipboard machines became the plague of space navigation. It reached the point where a gesture insufficiently polite, the slamming of a door, was enough to cause a shipboard refrigerator to rebel—which was exactly what happened with the notorious "Deepfreeze" on the transgalactic *Intrepid*. The name of Deepfreeze was repeated with horror for many years by the captains of the Milky Way lanes. This pirate was said to raid numerous ships, frighten passengers with its steel arms and icy breath, make off with sides of bacon, amass valuables and gold, and reportedly keep a whole harem of calculators, but it is not known how much truth there was to these and similar rumors. Its bloody career was ended finally by the well-aimed shot of an officer in the cosmic patrol. In reward, the officer, Constablomatic XG-17, was placed in the window of the New York branch of the Stellar Lloyd Agency, where he stands to this day.

While outer space was being filled with the din of battle and desperate SOS's from ships beset by electronic corsairs, in the big cities various masters of Electro-Jitsu or Judomatic made good money teaching self-defense courses, in which they showed how with a simple pair of pliers or a can opener one could disable the fiercest washing machine.

As we know, cranks and eccentrics are not confined to

any one time. In our day, too, there is no lack of them. From their ranks come individuals who proclaim theses contrary to common sense and prevailing opinion. One Cathodius Mattrass, a self-educated philosopher and born fanatic, founded the school of the so-called cyber-nophiles, which proclaimed the doctrine of cyber-nethics. According to this, the human race was intended by the Creator to serve as a kind of scaffolding, to be a means, a tool—for the creation of electrobrains more nearly perfect than itself. Mattrass's sect believed that the continued vegetation of the human race was a mis-understanding. The sect founded an order that devoted itself to the contemplation of electrical thought and did what it could to give refuge to robots in trouble. Cathodius himself, dissatisfied with the results of his endeavors, decided to take a radical step toward robots' liberation from human bondage. After consulting a number of eminent attorneys, he procured a rocket and flew to the nearby Crab Nebula. In empty regions fre-quented only by cosmic dust, he carried out unknown projects. Then the incredible affair of his heirs-successors came to light.

On the morning of August 29 all the papers carried this mysterious item: "Message from PASTA COSPOL VI/221: object measuring 520 mi × 80 mi × 37 mi dis-covered in Crab Nebula. Object executing movements similar to breast stroke. Further investigation in prog-ress."

The afternoon editions explained that the cosmic police patrol ship VI/221 had detected, at a distance of six light-weeks, a "man in the nebula." Closer examina-tion revealed that the "man" was a giant many hundreds of miles long and possessing a torso, head, arms, and legs, and that it was moving through a rarefied dust medium. Upon sighting the police ship, the giant first waved, then turned away.

Radio contact was soon established with the thing. It stated that it was the former Cathodius Mattrass, that after arriving two years ago at this place, it—he—had remade himself into robots, using, in part, the raw materials of the vicinity, and that in the future he would slowly but continually increase in size, because this suited him, and he asked to be left alone.

The commander of the patrol, pretending to take this statement at face value, concealed his ship behind a passing swarm of meteors. After a while he observed that the gigantic pseudo-human was gradually beginning to divide into much smaller pieces, each no larger than an average person, and that these parts or individuals were uniting to form something like a small round planet.

Coming out of hiding then, the commander asked the alleged Mattrass, by radio, what this spherical metamorphosis meant, and, also, what exactly was he—robot or human.

Mattrass replied that he assumed whatever shape he pleased, that he was not a robot, having arisen from a human, nor human, having rebuilt himself in robot form. He refused to give further explanations.

The case, to which the press gave considerable attention, gradually turned into a *cause célèbre*, because ships passing the Crab picked up snatches of radio conversations conducted by the so-called Mattrass; in these, he referred to himself as "Cathodius Sub One." It seemed that Cathodius Sub One—or Mattrass—was speaking to others (other robots?) as if conversing with his own hands and feet. The chatter in the region about Cathodius Sub One suggested that what one had here was a government established by either Mattrass or his robot derivatives. The State Department made a thorough investigation of the situation. The patrols reported that at times a metal sphere, at times a humanoid creature five hundred miles in length, was moving through the nebula, that it was speaking to itself about this and that, but concerning its statehood it gave evasive answers.

The authorities decided to put an immediate stop to the usurper's activity, but since the action would be (had to be) official, it was necessary to give it a name. Here the first obstacles arose. The MacFlacon Act, an annex to the civil code, dealt with movable property. In effect, electronic brains are considered movables, even when lacking legs. But here was a body the size of a planetoid in a nebula, and celestial bodies, though moving, are not considered movables. The question then came up whether or not a planet could be arrested; whether an assemblage of robots could be a planet; and, finally, whether this was one dismountable robot or a robot multitude.

Mattrass's legal adviser appeared before the authorities and submitted to them a statement from his client in which the latter declared that he was setting out for the Crab Nebula to transform himself into robots.

The initial interpretation of this datum, offered by the legal section of the State Department, went as follows: Mattrass, transforming himself into robots, had thereby destroyed his living organism and thus committed suicide. Which act was not punishable. The robot or robots that were a continuation of Mattrass, however, had been fabricated by the said individual and were therefore his property, and therefore now, after his demise, ought to devolve to the Treasury, since Mattrass had left no heir. On the basis of this decision, the State Department dispatched a bailiff to the nebula with the order to seize and seal everything he found there.

Mattrass's lawyer appealed, maintaining that the decision's acknowledgment of Mattrass's continuation ruled out suicide, because a person who continues exists, and if he exists, he has not committed suicide. Hence there were no "robots the property of Mattrass" but only Cathodius Mattrass, who had altered himself as he saw fit. Bodily alterations were not and could not be punished; nor was it lawful to impound the parts of a person's body—be they gold teeth or robots.

The State Department disagreed: from such an interpretation it followed that a living creature, in this instance a human being, could be built from obviously dead parts—robots. Then Mattrass's lawyer submitted to the authorities the deposition of a group of prominent physicists at Harvard, who testified unanimously that every living organism, the human organism included, is built of atomic particles, and these can only be regarded as dead.

Seeing that the case was taking a disturbing turn, the State Department gave up its attack on "Mattrass and successors" from the physio-biological standpoint and returned to the original decision, in which the word "continuation" was replaced by the word "product." The lawyer thereupon presented in court a new Mattrass statement, wherein the latter declared that the robots were in reality his children. The State Department demanded that adoption papers be produced—a ruse, since adoption of robots was not permitted by law. Mattrass's lawyer explained that actual paternity, not adoption, was the issue. The Department said that regulations required that children, to so qualify, have a father and a mother. The lawyer, prepared for this, added to the record the letter of one electrical engineer Melanie Fortinbras, who revealed that the birth of the parties in question had occurred in the course of her close collaboration with Mattrass.

The State Department questioned the nature of that collaboration as lacking "natural parental features." "In the aforementioned case," declared the government report, "one may speak of paternity or maternity in a figurative sense only, for the parentage involved is mental; whereas statutes require, for family law to come into effect, physical parentage."

Mattrass's lawyer demanded an explanation of how mental parentage differed from physical, and asked on what grounds the State Department regarded Cathodius Mattrass's union with Melanie Fortinbras as lacking physicality with respect to procreation.

The Department replied that the mental element in procreation, as recognized by and in accordance with the law, was negligible, whereas the physical predominated. Which latter did not occur in the case under discussion.

The lawyer then submitted the testimony of expert cybernetic midwives, indicating how greatly—in a physical sense—Cathodius and Melanie had to labor to bring into the world their autonomous offspring.

The Department finally decided to throw public decency aside and take a desperate step. It stated that the parental activities that causally and inevitably preceded the existence of children differed, in a fundamental way, from the programming of robots.

The lawyer was just waiting for this. He declared that children, too, were in a certain sense programmed by their parents in the course of their preparatory-preliminary activities; he asked the Department to describe precisely how, in its opinion, children should be conceived, that the act be in strict conformity with the law.

The Department, enlisting the aid of experts, prepared a voluminous reply, illustrated with plates and topographical diagrams, but since the main author of this so-called Pink Book was eighty-nine-year-old Professor Stockton-Mumford, the dean of American obstetrics, the lawyer immediately questioned his competence—in the area of causative-preparatory functions as regards parenthood—in view of the fact that, given his extremely advanced age, the professor must have lost all recollection of a number of details crucial to the case and was relying on rumors and the accounts of third parties.

The Department then undertook to substantiate the Pink Book with the sworn testimony of numerous fathers and mothers, but it was found that their statements differed considerably in places. About certain elements of the preliminary phase there was no agreement whatever. The Department, seeing that a fatal ambiguity was beginning to obscure this key issue, decided to question the material from which the alleged "children" of Mattrass and Fortinbras had been created, but then the rumor circulated (it was spread, they later discovered, by the lawyer) that Mattrass had ordered 450,000 tons of veal from Consolidated Corned Beef, Inc., and the Undersecretary of State dropped this plan in a hurry.

Instead, the Department, at the unfortunate suggestion of a theology professor, one Waugh, cited the Scripture. An unwise move, because Mattrass's lawyer parried with an exhaustive disquisition in which he proved, giving chapter and verse, that the Lord used only one part to program Eve, proceeding by a method most outlandish compared with that customarily employed by people, and yet He created a human being, for surely no one in his right mind considered Eve a robot. The Department then charged Mattrass and his successors with violating the MacFlacon Act, since as a robot (or robots) he had come into possession of a celestial body, and robots are forbidden ownership of planets or any other real estate.

This time the lawyer submitted to the Supreme Court all the documents that had been issued by the Department against Mattrass. First—he emphasized—it was evident, when one compared these texts, that in the State Department's view Mattrass was both his own father and his own son, and, at the same time, a celestial body. Second, the Department had misinterpreted the MacFlacon Act. The body of a certain individual, of Citizen Cathodius Mattrass, had been arbitrarily designated a planet. This conclusion was based on a legal, logical, and semantic absurdity.

That was how it began. Soon all the press wrote about was the "Celestial Body–Father–Son." The government commenced new legal actions, but each was nipped in the bud by Mattrass's indefatigable lawyer.

The State Department understood perfectly that Mattrass was not floating about in multiplied form in the Crab Nebula for the fun of it. No, his purpose was to create a legal precedent. Mattrass's going unpunished would have incalculable consequences, so the finest specialists pored over the record day and night, devising ever more tortuous juridical constructions, in the toils of which Mattrass was to meet his end. But each action was countered immediately by Mattrass's legal adviser. I myself followed the course of this struggle with keen interest. Then, unexpectedly, the Bar Association invited me to a special plenary session devoted to the problems of interpreting *"Casus* United States *contra* Cathodius Mattrass *alias* Cathodius Sub One *alias* the offspring of Mattrass and Fortinbras *alias* a planet in the Crab Nebula."

I was there at the designated time and place, and found the hall packed. The flower of the Bar filled tiers upon tiers of seats. The deliberations were already in progress. I sat in one of the last rows and began listening to the gray speaker.

"Distinguished colleagues!" he said, arms upraised. "Great difficulties await us when we proceed to a legal analysis of this problem! A certain Mattrass remakes himself into robots with the aid of a certain Fortinbras and at the same time enlarges himself on a scale of one to a million. That is how the matter looks to a layman, an ignoramus, a fool incapable of perceiving the abyss of legal problems that opens before our shocked eye! We must determine first of all with whom we are dealing—a human being, a robot, a government, a planet, children, a conspiracy, a demonstration, or an uprising. Consider how much depends on this decision. If, for example, we find that we are dealing not with a sovereign state but with a rebellious band of robots, a sort of electronic gang, then we are bound not by international law but by the common statutes regarding disorderly conduct in public places! If we rule that Mattrass, notwithstanding his multiplication, still exists and yet has children, it follows that this individual has given birth to himself—which causes the legal system terrible trouble, since we have no laws covering this, and *nulle crimen sine lege!* I therefore propose that Professor Ping Ling, the renowned authority on international law, be the first to take the floor!"

The venerable professor, greeted with warm applause, mounted the podium.

"Gentlemen," he said in an aged but powerful voice. "Let us consider first how a state is established. It is established in various ways, is it not? Our country, for example, was once an English colony; then it declared its independence and became a state. Does this occur in Mattrass's case? The answer is: if Mattrass, when remaking himself into robots, was of sound mind, then his state-creating act has legal validity, and we could define his nationality as electric. If, on the other hand, he was deranged, the act cannot be legally recognized."

Here an old man, grayer even than the first, jumped up in the middle of the hall and cried:

"High Court—I mean, gentlemen! I take the liberty of observing that if Mattrass was an insane state-creator, his descendants may still be sane; the state, which existed originally as a product of a private madness and thus had the nature of a morbid symptom, thereafter existed publicly, de facto, by the very consent of its electric inhabitants to the existing situation. And because no one can forbid the inhabitants of a state—who themselves have determined its legislative system—to acknowledge even the most insane authority (as has happened more than once in history), the existence of Mattrass's state de facto entails its existence de iure!!"

"My honorable opponent will forgive me," said Professor Ping Ling, "but Mattrass was our citizen, and consequently . . ."

"What of it?" shouted the irascible old man from the hall. "Either we recognize or we do not recognize Mattrass's state-creating act. If we recognize it and a sovereign state has arisen, then we have no claim against it. If, on the other hand, we do not recognize it, then either we are dealing with a corporate body or we are not. If we are not, if we do not have before us a legal entity, then the entire problem exists only for the sweepers of the Cosmic Trash Removal Agency, since there is a pile of scrap in the Crab Nebula—and our assembly has nothing at all to deliberate on! If, however, we have before us a legal entity, then another question arises. Sidereal law provides for the arrest, that is, the deprivation of freedom, of legal and physical entities on a planet or aboard a ship. The so-called Mattrass is not aboard a ship. On a planet, rather. We should therefore apply for his extradition. But there is no one to whom we can apply. Moreover, the planet on which he lives is himself. Therefore this place, considered from the only standpoint that concerns us—namely, the Majesty of the Law—constitutes a void, a kind of juridical nullity; but neither our civil law, nor our administrative law, nor our international law deals with nullities. Therefore, the remarks of esteemed Professor Ping Ling cannot shed light on the problem, because the problem does not exist!"

Having stunned the honorable assembly with this conclusion, the old man sat down.

During the next six hours I heard some twenty speakers; they showed, logically and irrefutably, that Mattrass existed, and that he did not exist; that he had established a state of robots, and that he was composed of such mechanical organisms; that he should be scrapped because he had broken a great number of laws, and that he had broken no law. Attorney Wurple's view that Mattrass was sometimes a planet, sometimes a robot, and sometimes nothing at all—a middle-of-the-road view meant to satisfy everyone—aroused general indignation and was supported by no one except its originator. But that was a trifle compared with the subsequent deliberations, for Senior Assistant Milger showed that Mattrass, by making himself into robots, had thereby multiplied his personality and now numbered about three hundred thousand. Because, however, there was no question of this collectivity representing a group of different individuals, since it was but one and the same individual repeated many times, Mattrass was a single entity in three hundred thousand aspects.

In reply Judge Hubble averred that the whole issue had been viewed incorrectly from the beginning: since Mattrass remade himself from a human being into robots, these robots were not he but someone else; since they were someone else, it was necessary to ascertain who they were; but if they were not human, they were no one; consequently, neither a juridical nor a physical problem existed, for there was no one whatsoever in the Crab Nebula.

I had already been painfully bumped around several times by the incensed participants. The security guards and the medical attendants had their hands full. Then suddenly cries rang out that electronic brains disguised as lawyers were present in the hall and should be removed at once, since their bias was indisputable—not to mention the fact that they had no right to take part in the deliberations. The chairman, Professor Claghorn, began walking about the hall with a small compass in hand; whenever its needle quivered and turned toward anyone seated in the audience, drawn by the iron hidden under his clothing, the individual was immediately unmasked and thrown out. In this way the hall was half emptied during the endless speeches of Professors Fitts,

Pitts, and Clabenti; the latter was interrupted in mid-sentence when the compass betrayed his electronic origin. After a short recess, during which we ate in the cafeteria to the increasing din of debate, I returned to the hall holding my jacket in place (all the buttons had been torn off by impassioned lawyers who had kept pulling me by the lapels)—and noticed a large X-ray machine near the podium. Attorney Plussek was speaking. He had just declared that Mattrass was a random cosmic phenomenon when the chairman marched up to me with a threatening look; the compass needle spun wildly in his palm. As the security guards collared me, I emptied my pockets of a penknife, a can opener, and a tea ball, and tore the nickel-plated buckles off my garters. No longer acting upon the magnetic needle, I was allowed to participate further in the deliberations. Forty throo moro had boon unmaskod as robots when Professor Dewey told us that Mattrass could be treated as a sort of cosmic aggregation. I was thinking that this had been said already—apparently the lawyers were running out of idoas—whon anothor inspection was made. Now all the participants were X-rayed unceremoniously, and it turned out that under their impeccably tailored suits they were hiding plastic, corundum, nylon, crystal, and even straw parts. Someone made of woolen yarn was reportedly discovered in one of the last rows. When the next speaker stepped down from the podium, I found myself conspicuously alone in the middle of the huge hall. The speaker was X-rayed and immediately thrown out. Then the chairman, the last person besides me to remain, approached my chair. All of a sudden—I don't know why—I took the compass from his hand; it whirled accusingly and pointed at him. I tapped his belly with a knuckle, and it rang. Without thinking I seized him by the scruff of the neck and threw him out. I stood facing several hundred abandoned briefcases, thick folders with documents, canes, derbies and other hats, leather-bound books, and galoshes. Pacing the empty hall for a while and seeing that there was nothing for me to do there, I turned sharply and went home.

Doctor Diagoras

Unable to take part in the XVIIIth International Cybernetic Congress, I tried following it in the newspapers. This was not easy, since reporters have a talent for distorting scientific data. It was only thanks to them, however, that I made the acquaintance of Doctor Diagoras, for they turned his speech into the sensation of the slack season. Even if the professional journals had been at my disposal, I would never have learned of the existence of that peculiar individual: he was merely named in the list of participants, and the text of his lecture was left out. I learned from the papers that his speech had been disgraceful, and that had it not been for the tactfulness of the presiding officers, a brawl would have resulted. This unknown, self-styled reformer of science had heaped abuse on the most eminent authorities and, when ruled out of order, had smashed the microphone with his cane. The epithets he hurled at the luminaries present were reproduced almost verbatim by the press, but the speech itself was so totally passed over that my curiosity was aroused.

When I returned home, I looked up Doctor Diagoras but could not find his name either in the *Cybernetic Problems* yearbooks or in the latest edition of *Who's Who*. So I called Professor Corcoran. Corcoran said he did not know the "madman's" address, but would not give it to me even if he did. That was all I needed to take a serious interest in Diagoras. I placed a number of queries in the classifieds, and to my amazement met with instant success. I received a letter, dry and concise, written in a rather unfriendly tone; the doctor agreed to receive me "on his estate" in Crete. The map indicated that the estate was no more than sixty miles from the place of the legendary Minotaur.

A cyberneticist with his own estate in Crete, engaged in solitary, mysterious research! That same afternoon I flew to Athens. There was no further flight connection, so I boarded a ship and arrived at the island the next morning. I rented a car. The road was terrible—as was the heat. The surrounding hills were the color of burnt copper. The car, my duffel bag, my clothes, and finally my face were covered with dust.

During the last few miles I did not come across a living soul; there was no one I could ask for directions. Diagoras had told me in the letter to stop at the thirtieth milestone, because I would be unable to drive any farther, so I parked the car in the meager shade of some umbrella pines and began penetrating the dense brush on foot. The ground was overgrown with typical Mediterranean vegetation, so unattractive up close. It was out of the question to turn off any path; my clothes would have caught immediately on the sun-scorched brambles. I wandered over the stony trails for nearly three hours, bathed in sweat. I cursed myself for a fool. What did I care about the man and his story? I had set out at noon, when the heat was greatest, and since I had gone without lunch, I now began to feel pangs of hunger. I finally returned to the car. It had already emerged from the narrow strip of shade. The leather seats seared like an oven, and the whole interior reeked with the nauseous odor of gasoline and heated paint.

Suddenly a lone sheep appeared from around the bend. It came up to me, bleated in a humanlike voice, and toddled off to one side. As it was disappearing from view, I noticed a narrow path running up a slope. I expected to see a shepherd, but the sheep disappeared and no one came along.

Although the sheep was not a particularly trustworthy guide, I got out of the car again and began pushing through the brush. Soon the way became easier. It was already growing dark when, beyond a small lemon grove, there loomed the outline of a large building. The thickets gave way to grass so dry that it rustled underfoot like charred paper. The house, shapeless, dark, and exceedingly ugly, with the ruins of a portal, was surrounded in a wide radius by a high wire fence. The sun was setting and I still could not find an entrance. I began calling loudly, but with no result—all the windows were shuttered. I was losing hope that there was anyone inside when the gate opened and a man appeared.

He gestured to me the way to go; the wicket was in such a dense clump of bushes that I never would have suspected its existence. Protecting my face from the branches, I managed to reach it; it had already been opened with a key. The man who had opened it looked like a mechanic or a butcher. He was a paunchy, short-necked individual with a sweaty skullcap on his bald head. He wore no jacket, only a long oilskin apron over a shirt with rolled-up sleeves.

"Excuse me—does Doctor Diagoras live here?" I asked. He looked up at me with an expressionless face, large, misshapen, and puffy. The face of a butcher. But his eyes were bright and razor-sharp. Though he said not a word, I could tell from his glance that it was he.

"Excuse me," I repeated, "you're Doctor Diagoras, aren't you?"

He gave me his hand. It was as small and soft as a woman's, but it gripped mine with unexpected strength. He flexed the skin of his head, causing the skullcap to slide back, stuck both his hands in his apron pockets, and asked me with a shade of contempt:

"Just what do you want from me?"

"Nothing," I shot back. I had undertaken this journey on the spur of the moment, wanting to meet this extraordinary person, and was prepared for almost anything. But I would not put up with insults. I was giving thought to my return trip as he stared at me, went on staring, and finally said:

"I guess it's all right. Follow me."

It was now evening. He took me to the gloomy mansion and entered a dim hall; when I stepped inside behind him I heard an echo, as if we stood in the nave of a church. Diagoras made his way through this darkness with ease. He did not warn me about the staircase step, and I tripped. Cursing to myself, I went up the stairs toward the faint light of a half-open door.

We entered a room with a single, shuttered window. The shape of this room, especially its unusually high, arched ceiling, reminded me more of the interior of a tower than of a home. It was crammed with huge, dark pieces of furniture, their polish dulled by age, including chairs with uncomfortably sculptured backs. On the walls hung oval miniatures, and in the corner stood a clock, a monstrous thing with a dial of burnished copper and a pendulum the size of a Hellenic shield.

The room was quite dark; the light bulbs in an intricate lamp with dusty shades barely illuminated a square table. The somber walls, covered with reddish-brown paper, absorbed the light, keeping the corners of the room black. Diagoras stood by the table, his hands in his apron pockets. It seemed as if we were waiting for something. I had just put my duffel bag on the floor when the great clock began ringing out the hour. In a clear, loud tone it struck eight; then something in it grated, and an old man's voice exclaimed:

"Diagoras, you scoundrel! Where are you? How dare you treat me this way! Speak to me, do you hear?! For God's sake, Diagoras . . . there's a limit!" Both rage and despair trembled in these words. But what surprised me most was that I recognized the voice; it belonged to Professor Corcoran.

"If you don't speak . . ." the voice threatened, but suddenly the clockwork grated again and fell silent.

"What . . ." I said. "Did you put a phonograph in there? Why do you waste your time on such games?"

My intenion was to nettle him. But Diagoras, as though not hearing me, pulled a cord, and the same gruff voice filled the room:

"Diagoras, you'll regret this, you can be certain! No matter what you've been through, you have no excuse for abusing me. If you think I'd stoop to beg . . ."

"You already have," Diagoras said nonchalantly.

"That's a lie. You're a scoundrel, an arrant scoundrel, unworthy of the name of scientist! The world will learn of your . . ."

The toothed gears turned, and again there was silence.

"A phonograph?" Diagoras sneered. "A phonograph, you say? No, my dear sir. The chime contains Professor Corcoran *in persona*, or, rather, *in spiritu suo*. I have immortalized him for my own amusement. What is wrong with that?"

"How do you mean?" I stammered. The fat man considered whether I was worth an answer.

"I mean it literally," he said at last. "I reconstituted all his personality traits, modeled them into a suitable system, miniaturized his soul electronically, and thus obtained an exact portrait of that famous person, which I installed in this clock. . . ."

"You say it's not just a recorded voice?"

He shrugged.

"Try it yourself. Have a chat with him, although he's not in the best of moods—but in his circumstances that's understandable. You wish to talk to him?" He pointed to the cord. "Go ahead."

"No," I replied. What was this? Madness? A macabre joke? Revenge?

"But the real Corcoran is in his laboratory right now, on the continent," I added.

"Of course. This is only his mental portrait. But it's perfectly faithful, in no way inferior to the original."

"Why did you make it?"

"I needed it. Once I had to construct a model of the human brain; that was a preliminary step to another, more difficult problem. The person was of no importance here. I chose Corcoran—who knows?—because it struck my fancy. He had created so many thinking machines himself—I thought it would be amusing to shut him up in one of them, particularly in the role of a chime."

"Does he know . . . ?" I asked quickly as Diagoras turned toward the door.

"Yes," he replied indifferently. "I even made it possible for him to talk to himself—by telephone. But enough. I didn't intend to show off; it was a coincidence that the clock struck eight when you came."

With mixed feelings I followed him down a dim corridor. Along its walls stood cobweb-covered metal skeletons, resembling those of prehistoric amphibians. The corridor ended at a door, behind which lay darkness. I heard the click of a switch. We were on a winding stone staircase. Diagoras went first, his ducklike shadow moving across the wall. We stopped at a metal door, which he opened with a key. A gust of stale, warm air hit me in the face. A light went on. We were not—contrary to what I had expected—in a laboratory. If that long room with an aisle down the middle resembled anything, it would be the menagerie of a traveling circus. There were cages on either side. I walked behind Diagoras, who, in his sweaty shirt, the apron strings crossed on his back, looked like an animal trainer.

The cages were closed off by wire netting. In the dark cells behind it loomed indistinct shapes—machines? presses?—at any rate, not living creatures. Yet I instinctively sniffed, as though expecting an odor of wild animals. But the air held only the smell of chemicals, heated oil, and rubber.

On the next cells the netting was so close-meshed that I thought of birds—what other creatures had to be confined so tightly? Then I passed cages on which there were grilles instead of wire netting. A lot like a zoo, where one goes from birds and monkeys to cages containing wolves and the great predators.

The last compartment was provided with two grilles separated by some two feet of open space. One finds such grilles on the cages of particularly ferocious animals, to keep unwary people from approaching too closely and being clawed. Diagoras halted, put his face up to the grille, and tapped on it with his key. I peered inside. Something was resting in the far corner, but I could not make out its contours in the dim light. Suddenly a shapeless mass shot toward us before I had time even to flinch. The grille clanged as though struck with a hammer. I jumped back. Diagoras did not even budge. Opposite his calm face hung a monster, a shiny metal hulk, a cross between an insect abdomen and a skull. The skull, indescribably hideous and at the same time manlike, stared at Diagoras so intently, so greedily, that my skin crawled. The grille it clung to quivered slightly, revealing the power with which it pressed against the bars. Diagoras, apparently quite certain that they would hold, looked at this inexplicable creature as a gardener or a breeder might regard a particularly successful hybrid. The steel hulk slid down the grille with a terrible screech and became motionless, and the cage appeared empty again.

Without a word Diagoras moved on. I followed, quite stunned, though beginning to understand. But the explanation that came to my mind was so farfetched, I dismissed it. The man gave me no time to think, however. He stopped.

"No, Tichy," he said quietly. "I don't build them for pleasure, nor do I desire their hatred. I'm not concerned about my children's feelings . . . they were simply experimental stages, necessary stages. An explanation is in order, but to make it short I'll start in the middle. . . . Do you know what constructors demand from their cybernetic creations?"

Without giving me time to think he answered the question himself:

"Obedience. They never talk about it, and some may not even be aware of it, because it's a tacit assumption. A fatal mistake! They build a machine and insert a program it must carry out, whether the program is a math problem or a sequence of controlled actions—in an automated factory, for example. A fatal mistake, I say, because to obtain immediate results they exclude the possibility of spontaneous behavior in their creations. Understand me, Tichy, the obedience of a hammer, a lathe, or a computer is basically the same thing—and that is not what we were after! The difference here is one only of degree; you guide the blows of a hammer directly, while you program a computer without knowing its process as exactly as that of a primitive tool. But cybernetics promised thought—in other words, autonomy, the relative independence of the system from man! The best-trained dog may not obey its master, but no one then will say that the dog is 'defective,' yet that is exactly what they call a computer that operates contrary to its program. . . . But why speak of dogs? The nervous system of a beetle no larger than a pin shows spontaneity; why, even an ameba has its whims, its unpredictable behavior. Without such unpredictability there is no cybernetics. An understanding of this simple matter is really everything. All else"—he indicated the silent hall and the rows of dark cages with a sweeping gesture—"all else is only a consequence."

"I don't know how familiar you are with Corcoran's work—" I began, and broke off, remembering the "chime."

"Don't bother me with him!" He bridled and thrust his fists into his apron pockets. "Corcoran, my dear sir, fell prey to a common fallacy. He wanted to philosophize, that is, to play God; for what is philosophy, in the end, but the desire to understand things to a degree greater than science permits? Philosophy wants to answer all questions, like a God. Corcoran tried to become God; cybernetics for him was merely a tool, a means of accomplishing his purpose. I want only to be a man, Tichy, nothing more. But that's precisely why I've gone further than Corcoran. He was so intent on his goal that he immediately limited himself; he set up a pseudo-human world in his machines; he created a clever imitation, nothing more. If that were my goal, I could create any world I pleased . . . but what's the use of plagiarisms. . . . And maybe one day I'll do it. But for the time being I have other problems. You've heard about my rowdiness? You needn't answer, I know you have. That stupid reputation of mine brought you here. It's nonsense, Tichy. I was simply annoyed by the blindness of those people. But, gentlemen—I told them—if I present you with a machine that extracts square roots from even numbers but doesn't want to from odd numbers, that's no defect, damn it, that's an achievement! A machine has idiosyncrasies, tastes, already shows something like a rudimentary free will, the seed of spontaneity—and you say it must be rebuilt! Of course it must, but in such a way as to increase its capriciousness. . . . Meanwhile . . . it's impossible to talk to people who cannot see the obvious. The Americans are working on a perceptron, Tichy—they think that's the way to build an intelligent machine. That's the way to build an electronic slave! I put my money on the sovereignty, the independence of my constructions. Needless to say, it didn't go smoothly; I was perplexed at first; there were times I even doubted that I was right. This happened then."

He rolled up a sleeve; above the biceps was a whitish scar as large as a palm, surrounded by a pink welt.

"The first manifestations of spontaneity were not

pleasant. They didn't arise from intelligence. You cannot build an intelligent machine straight off. It would be like someone in ancient Greece wanting to go from quadrigae to jet planes. You cannot skip stages of evolution—even if it's a cybernetic evolution begun by us. This first pupil of mine"—he put his hand on his mutilated arm—"had less 'intelligence' than any beetle. But it showed spontaneity, and how!"

"One moment," I said. "You're saying strange things. Haven't you already built an intelligent machine? It's in that clock."

"That's precisely what I call plagiarizing!" he replied vehemently. "A new myth has arisen, Tichy, the myth of building a 'homunculus.' Just why should we build people out of transistors and glass? Perhaps you can explain it to me? Is an atomic pile a synthetic star? Is a dynamo an artificial storm? Why should an intelligent machine be a 'synthetic brain' created in the image and likeness of man? For what purpose? To add, to these three billion proteinaceous beings, yet another, but one made of plastic and copper? That's fine as a circus stunt, but not as a cybernetic creation."

"What is it, then, you want to build?"

He smiled unexpectedly, and his face, amazingly, became that of a willful child.

"Tichy . . . now you'll surely take me for a madman: I don't know what I want!"

"I don't understand. . . ."

"But at least I know what I don't want. I don't want to repeat the human brain. Nature had her reasons for constructing it—biological, adaptational, etc. She worked in the ocean and in the branches where apemen climbed, amid fangs, claws, and blood, between the stomach and the sexual organs. But how does that concern me as a *constructor*? Now you see who you're dealing with. But I don't despise the human brain at all, Tichy, as that old fool Barness accused. Studying it is extremely important, absolutely vital, and if someone wants, I can immediately pay my humblest respects to that magnificent creation of nature!"

The professor really did make a bow.

"Does that mean, however, that I must imitate it? All of them, the poor devils, are certain I must! Imagine a group of Neanderthals who have their own cave and need nothing else! They don't care to know what it's like having houses, churches, amphitheaters, any buildings at all, because they have a cave and will go on hollowing out the same caves forever!"

"All right, then, but you must be striving for something. Heading in some direction. Therefore you expect something. What? Construction of a genius . . .?"

Diagoras looked at me with his head tilted, and his beady eyes suddenly became mocking.

"You sound just like them," he said finally in a quiet voice. " 'What does he want? To build a genius? A superman?' You ass, if I don't want to plant McIntoshes does that mean I'm condemned to Winesaps? Are there only small apples and big apples, or could there be a whole vast class of fruits? From among the unimaginable number of *possible* systems, nature built just one— the one she realized in us. Because it was the best system, you think? But since when does nature strive for Platonic perfection? She built what she could, period. Neither constructing Eniacs—or other calculating machines—nor imitating the brain will get you anywhere. From Eniacs you can go only to other, still more rapid mathematical cretins. As for plagiarisms of the brain, one can produce them, but that's not the most important thing. Please forget everything you've heard about cybernetics. My 'kybernoidea' and I have nothing in common with it except a common beginning. But that's an old story now, because this stage"—again he indicated the dead-silent hall— "is behind me. I keep these freaks ... I don't know why ... perhaps out of sentimentality. ..."

"Then you're exceptionally sentimental," I mumbled with an involuntary glance at his arm.

"Perhaps. If you want to see another of the closed chapters of my work, follow me."

We descended the winding stone staircase, passed the first floor, and went down into the basement. There, under a low ceiling, burned lamps in wire caps. Diagoras opened a heavy steel door. We found ourselves in a square, windowless room. In the middle of the cement floor, which sloped as if toward a catch basin, I saw a round, cast-iron, padlocked hatch. I was surprised that the basin was shut in this way. Diagoras opened the padlock, gripped the iron handle, and with a twist of his fat body lifted the heavy lid. I leaned over beside him and looked down. The steel-lined opening was closed off from below by a thick plate of wired glass. Through this great lens I could see the interior of a spacious bunker. On the bottom of it, amid an indescribable chaos of charred metal cables and rubble, there rested, covered with plaster dust and crushed glass, a torpid, dark mass that resembled the body of a split octopus. I glanced at Diagoras's face; he was smiling.

"This experiment might have cost me dearly," he confessed, straightening his corpulent figure. "I wanted to introduce into cybernetic evolution a principle unknown in biological evolution: I wanted to build an organism endowed with the capacity for self-complication. That is, if the task it sets itself (I did not know what that might be) proves too difficult, then it can reconstruct itself. Down there I kept eight hundred elementary electronic blocks that were able to combine with one another freely, according to the rules of permutation...."

"And you succeeded?"

"All too well. I'm not sure what pronoun to use here; let's say *he*"—Diagoras pointed to the torpid monster— "decided to escape. That's generally their first impulse, you know...." He broke off and stared into space, as though surprised by his own words. "I don't understand why, but their spontaneous activity always begins in this way; they want to free themselves, to break loose from the restrictions I impose on them. I can't tell you what they would do after that, because I never permitted it. Perhaps my fears were a little exaggerated.

"I was careful, or at least I thought so. This bunker ... the contractor I had make it must have been amazed, but I paid him well and he asked no questions. Five feet of reinforced concrete ... and the walls were steel-plated, not with rivets—rivets are too easy to tear out—but welded electrically. Twenty-three centimeters of the best armor plate I could obtain, from an old battleship. Why don't you take a closer look?"

I knelt at the edge of the shaft and leaned over to see the bunker wall. The armor plate was ripped apart from top to bottom and bent like the sides of a huge tin can. Between its jagged edges yawned a deep hole, from which protruded wires studded with chunks of cement.

"He did that ... ?" I asked, unconsciously lowering my voice.

"Yes."

"How?"

"I don't know. I did build him out of steel, but I purposely used soft steel, not tempered. Moreover, there were no tools in the bunker. I can only guess. Whether I did it out of foresight I can't say, but I had reinforced the ceiling particularly well with a triple layer of armorplate. And the glass cost me a fortune. It's the kind used in bathyscaphes. Not even an armor-piercing shell can break it. I think that's why he didn't spend much time on it. I assume he produced a sort of induction furnace in which he tempered his head—or maybe he induced currents in the wall plates themselves—I tell you I don't know. When I observed him he behaved quite calmly; he bustled about in there, combined things. . . ."

"Were you able to communicate with him in any way?"

"How could I? His intelligence, for all I know, was on the level of a lizard's—at least initially. How far he advanced I can't tell you, because I was more interested then in how to destroy him than in asking him questions."

"What did you do?"

"It was at night. I awoke with the impression that the whole house was starting to collapse. He had cut through the armor plate instantly, but the concrete required work. By the time I had run here, he was already halfway in the hole. In half an hour at the most, he would reach the ground under the foundation and pass through it like butter. I had to act fast."

"You turned off the electricity?"

"Immediately. But without result."

"Impossible!"

"Yet true. I wasn't careful enough. I knew where the power line supplying the house was, but it hadn't occurred to me that there might be a deeper line. There was, and he reached it and became independent of my circuit breakers."

"But that presupposes intelligent behavior!"

"Nothing of the kind; it's an ordinary tropism. A plant grows toward the light, an infusorian moves toward a concentration of hydrogen ions; he looked for electricity. The power I had supplied him with wasn't enough, so he sought another source."

"And what did you do?"

"At first I was going to call the power station, or at least the substation, but that would have revealed my projects and perhaps made it difficult to continue them. I used liquid oxygen; luckily I had some. My whole supply went in there."

"He was paralyzed by the low temperature?"

"It did not so much paralyze him as destroy his coordination. He thrashed about. . . . I tell you, that was a sight! I had to hurry—I didn't know whether he would adapt to the bath, too—so I didn't waste time pouring out the oxygen, but threw it in together with the Dewar vessels."

"Vacuum bottles?"

"Yes, they're like large vacuum bottles."

"Ah, that's why there's so much glass."

"Exactly. He smashed everything within reach. An epileptic fit . . . It's hard to believe—the house is old and has two stories, but it shook. I felt the floor tremble."

"What happened next?"

"I had to render him harmless before the temperature rose. I couldn't go down myself—I would have frozen instantly. Nor could I use explosives; I didn't want to blow up my home, after all. When he had stopped rampaging and was only quivering, I opened the hatch and let down a small robot with a carborundum circular saw."

"Didn't the robot freeze?"

"About eight times. I would pull it out—it was tied to a rope. But each time it cut deeper. Finally it destroyed him."

"Gruesome," I muttered.

"No, cybernetic evolution. But perhaps I go in for theatrical effects, and that's why I showed you this. Let's go back."

Wih these words Diagoras lowered the armored hatch.

"There's one thing I don't understand," I said. "Why do you expose yourself to such dangers? You must enjoy them; otherwise . . ."

"Et tu, Brute?" he replied, pausing on the first step. "What else could I have done, in your opinion?"

"You could have constructed electronic brains only, without limbs, armor, or effectors. They would be incapable of anything except mental activity."

"That was my very goal, though I was unable to realize it. Chains of proteins can combine on their own, but not transistors or cathode tubes. I had to provide 'limbs.' A poor solution, because—only because—it was a primitive one. There are other forms of danger, you see."

He turned and went upstairs. We found ourselves on the first floor, but this time Diagoras headed in the opposite direction. He stopped in front of a copper-plated door.

"When I spoke of Corcoran, you no doubt thought that I envy him. I don't. Corcoran wasn't seeking knowledge; he merely wanted to create what he had planned, and since he made only what he wanted, what he could comprehend, he learned nothing and proved nothing except that he is a skillful technician. I am much less confident than Corcoran. I say: I don't know, but I want to know. Building a manlike machine, a grotesque rival for the good things of this world, would be ordinary imitation."

"But every construction must be what you create it to be," I protested. "You may not know its future activity exactly, but you must have an initial plan."

"Not at all. I told you about the first, spontaneous reaction of my kybernoids—the attacking of obstacles and limitations. Don't think that I or anyone else will ever know where this comes from, why this is so."

"*Ignoramus et ignorabimus* . . .?"

"Yes. I'll prove it to you now. We ascribe mental life to other people because we possess it ourselves. The further removed an animal is from man with respect to structure and function, the less certain our assumptions about its mental life. We ascribe definite emotions to monkeys, dogs, and horses, but we know very little about the 'experiences' of a lizard. With insects or infusorians, analogies become futile. We shall never know whether a certain pattern of neural stimulation in the thoracic brain of an ant is accompanied by 'joy' or 'anxiety,' or whether the ant can experience such states at all. Now, what is relatively unimportant concerning animals—the problem of the existence or nonexistence of their mental life—becomes a nightmare when we deal with kybernoids. No sooner do they rise from the dead than they fight to liberate themselves, but why this happens and what subjective state accompanies these violent efforts—this we shall never know."

"If they begin to talk . . ."

"Our language arose in the course of social evolution and conveys information about analogous—or similar—states, for we all resemble one another. Because our brains are alike, you suspect that when I laugh, I feel what you feel when you're in a good mood. But you can't say that about them. Pleasures? Feelings? Fear? What happens to the meaning of such words when they are transferred from a blood-fed human brain to a row of electrical coils? And what if even those coils are absent, if the constructional similarity is done away with completely—what then? If you want to know: the experiment has already been carried out."

He opened the door we had been standing in front of. We entered a large, white room lit by four lamps. It was warm and close, like a greenhouse. In the middle of the tile floor rose a wide metal cylinder from which thin pipes sprouted in various directions. A large, bulging lid hermetically sealed with a screw wheel gave it the appearance of a fermentation vat. On its sides were smaller portholes, round and tightly shut. The cylinder—I noticed this now—rested not on the floor but on a platform made of sheets of cork interlaid with sponge mats.

Diagoras opened one of the side portholes and pointed; I leaned over and peeked inside. What I saw defied all description. Behind the thick round glass spread a viscous structure consisting of thick stalks and gossamer bridges and festoons. The whole mass, completely motionless, remained mysteriously suspended: to judge from the consistency of that pulp or ooze, it should have sunk to the bottom of the tank. Through the glass I felt a light pressure on my face, as if from hot, stagnant air; I even smelled—though it might have been my imagination—the delicate, sickly-sweet odor of decay. The oozy substance shone as if there were a light

somewhere within it or above it, and its thinnest fila-
ments had a silvery gleam. Suddenly I noticed a slight
movement. One gray-brown tentacle covered with pus-
tular swellings rose and glided, through the loops of
others, in my direction. With peristaltic spasms, as of
slimy, repulsive intestines, it came up to the glass,
pressed against it opposite my face, and made several
feeble crawling motions before becoming still. I had the
eerie feeling that this jelly was looking at me. A
thoroughly disagreeable feeling, yet I was unable to pull
away, as though out of shame. At that moment I forgot
about Diagoras, who was watching me from the side,
and about everything I had experienced thus far. With
growing bewilderment I stared at the fungous ooze,
absolutely certain that what faced me was not just a
living substance but a real being. Why, I cannot say.

Nor do I know how long I would have stood and stared
had it not been for Diagoras, who took me gently by the
arm, closed the porthole, and turned the screw wheel
hard.

"What is it?" I asked, as if he had wakened me. Only
now came my reaction; it was with nausea and confusion that I looked at the fat scientist and the hot copper
tank.

"A fungoid," replied Diagoras. "The dream of cy-
berneticists—a self-organizing substance. I had to give
up traditional materials. This one proved better. It's a
polymer."

"Is it—alive?"

"What can I tell you? It has neither protein, nor cells,
nor metabolism. I accomplished this after an enormous
number of tests. To put it briefly, I initiated a chemical
evolution. Selection was to give rise to a substance that
would react to every external stimulus with internal

change, not only to neutralize the stimulus but to free itself from it. First I exposed the substance to heat, magnetic fields, and radiation. But that was just the beginning. I gave it increasingly difficult tasks; for example, I used definite patterns of electric shocks from which it could free itself only by producing a specific rhythm of currents in reply. . . . In this way I taught it conditioned reflexes, so to speak. But that, too, was a preliminary phase. It soon began to universalize; it solved increasingly difficult problems."

"How is that possible, if it has no senses?"

"To tell the truth, I don't understand it fully myself. I can only give you the principle. If you put a computer on a cybernetic 'tortoise' and let it into a big hall, equipped with a quality-of-function regulator, you will obtain a system devoid of 'senses' but which reacts to any change in the environment. If there is a magnetic field somewhere in the hall exerting a negative effect on the operation of the computer, it will immediately withdraw and search for a spot where such disturbances do not occur. The constructor need not even anticipate every possible disturbance, which may be mechanical vibrations, heat, loud sounds, the presence of electrical charges—anything. The machine does not 'perceive,' because it has no senses, so it does not feel heat or see light, but it reacts as though it does see and feel. Now, that's only an elementary model. The fungoid"—he put his hand on the copper cylinder, which reflected his image like a grotesquely distorting mirror—"can do that and a thousand times more. My idea was to create a liquid medium filled with 'constructional elements,' from which the original organization could draw and build as it wished. That's how the fungoid arose."

"But what is it exactly? A brain?"

"I can't tell you that; we have no words for it. To our way of thinking it isn't a brain, since it doesn't belong to any living creature, nor was it constructed to solve definite problems. However, I assure you it thinks—though not like an animal or a human being."

"How do you know that?"

"It's a long story. Allow me. . . ."

He opened a door that was metal-plated and extremely thick, almost like the door of a bank vault; the other side was covered with sheets of cork and the same spongy material that supported the copper cylinder. In the next, smaller room there was also a light; the window was blocked with black paper, and on the floor, away from the walls, stood the same type of red copper vat.

"You have two . . . ?" I asked, stunned. "But why?"

"A variant," he replied, closing the door. I noticed how carefully he did so.

"I didn't know which of them would function better. There are important differences in chemical structure and so on. . . . I did have others, but they were no good. Only these two passed through all the stages of the selection process. They developed very nicely," he went on, putting his hand on the convex lid of the second cylinder, "but I didn't know whether that meant anything. They became quite independent of changes in their environment; both were able to guess quickly what I demanded of them—in other words, to react in a way that freed them from harmful stimuli. Surely you'll admit that it's something"—he turned toward me with unexpected vehemence—"if a gelatinous paste can solve with electrical impulses an equation given it by means of other electrical impulses. . . .?"

"Of course, but as for thinking . . ."

"Maybe it's not thinking," he replied. "Names are not important here; the facts are. After a while both began to show increasing—what should I call it?—indifference to my stimuli, unless their actual existence was threatened. Yet my sensing devices registered exceptionally intense activity during this time, in the form of series of discharges."

He took from the drawer of a small table a strip of photographic paper with an irregular sinusoidal line.

"Series of such 'electrical attacks' occurred in both fungoids, apparently without any external cause. I began to study the matter more systematically and discovered a strange phenomenon: *that* one"—he pointed to the door leading to the larger room—"produced electromagnetic waves, and *this* one received them. When I realized that, I noticed at once that their activity alternated; one was 'silent' while the other 'broadcast.' "

"What are you saying?!"

"The truth. I immediately shielded both rooms—did you notice the sheet metal on the doors? The walls are also covered with it, but they are painted. This prevented radio contact. The activity of both fungoids increased, then fell almost to zero after a few hours. But the next day it was the same as before. Do you know what happened? They had switched to ultrasonic vibrations—they sent signals through the walls and ceilings. . . ,"

"That's why you have the cork!"

"Exactly. I could have destroyed them, of course, but what good would that have done me? I placed both containers on sound-absorbing insulation. In this way I broke off their communication again. Then they started growing . . . until they reached their present size. They became almost four times larger."

"Why?"

"I have no idea."

Diagoras stood by the metal cylinder. He did not look at me; as he spoke, he repeatedly put his hand on the arched lid, as though to check the temperature.

"Their electrical activity returned to normal after a few days, as if they had succeeded in re-establishing contact. I eliminated thermal and radioactive radiation, installed every possible shield, screen, and proofing, used ferromagnetic sensors—all to no avail. I even moved this one down to the basement for a week, then took it out to a shed, which you might have seen—it's a hundred feet from the house. But their activity during the whole time did not undergo the slightest change. The 'questions' and 'answers' that I registered and which I am still registering"—he pointed to the oscillograph under the shaded window—"have gone on continuously in series, night and day. They work incessantly. I tried to break in on their signaling with false 'messages.' "

"You faked the signals? Then you know what they mean?"

"Not for the life of me. But you can record on tape what one person says in an unknown language and replay it for someone else who also speaks that language. That's what I tried to do, and failed. They still send each other the same impulses, those damned signals—but in what manner, I have no idea."

"It could be an independent, spontaneous activity," I observed. "You have no conclusive proof, after all."

"In a sense I do. You see, the time is also recorded on the tapes. Thus a clear correlation exists: when one is broadcasting the other is silent, and vice versa. Lately the intervals have increased considerably, but the pattern hasn't changed. Do you realize what I've done? One can guess the plans, the good or bad intentions, the innermost thoughts of a silent person from his facial expression and his behavior. But my creations have no face or body—just as you postulated before—and now I stand helpless, without a chance of understanding. Should I destroy them? That would be an admission of failure! They don't want contact with man—or is that as impossible as contact between an ameba and a turtle? I don't know. I don't know anything!"

He stood by the gleaming cylinder, his hand on its lid. It was no longer me he was speaking to; he could even have forgotten I was there. Nor did I hear his last words—my attention had been drawn by something odd. As he spoke, with increasing vehemence, he kept lifting his right hand and placing it on the copper surface; something about the hand seemed not right. Its movement was unnatural. Whenever his fingers came near the metal, they shook for a second—shook rapidly, unlike a nervous tremor. But before, when he gestured, his movement had been steady and decisive, with no trace of shakiness. I looked at his hand more closely now; amazed and shocked, yet hoping that I was mistaken, I stammered:

"Diagoras, what is wrong with your hand?"

"What? What hand?" He looked at me in surprise. I had interrupted his train of thought.

"That," I pointed. He brought his hand near the shiny surface. It began shaking. Open-mouthed, he held it up to his eyes. The shaking immediately stopped. Once more he looked at his hand, then at me, and very cautiously, millimeter by millimeter, brought it up to the metal. When the fingertips touched the surface, the muscles started twitching slightly, and the twitching spread to the entire hand. He stood still, an indescribable expression on his face. Then he clenched his fist, propped it on his hip, and moved his elbow toward the copper surface. The muscles of the forearm twitched where the skin came in contact with the cylinder. He stepped back, raised his hands to his eyes, and examined them in turn, whispering: "So it was I . . .? I myself . . . through me. . . then I was . . . the subject of the experiment . . ."

I thought he would burst into hysterical laughter, but he thrust his hands into his apron pockets, walked silently across the room, and said in a changed voice:

"I don't know whether that has any—but enough. You'd better go now. I have nothing else to show, and besides . . ."

He broke off, went up to the window, tore away the black paper covering it, and threw open the shutters. Breathing loudly, he looked out into the darkness.

"Why don't you go?" he mumbled without turning around. "That would be best."

I did not want to leave like that. The scene, which later, in my memory, would strike me as grotesque—the copper vat filled with those oozing intestines that had turned his body into an involuntary messenger of unknown signals—at that moment horrified me and filled me with pity for the man. That is why I would prefer to end my story here. For what happened afterward was senseless: his outburst against me, that I had—he said—intruded; his angry face, the insults and the shouting—all that, and the submissive silence with which I left, seemed like a clichéd nightmare. To this day I do not know whether he threw me out of his gloomy house because he *wanted* to or whether . . .

But I could be wrong. Possibly both of us then were

the victims of a delusion, and we hypnotized each other. Such things do happen.

But, then, how is one to explain the discovery made quite accidentally about a month after my Cretan expedition? While investigating a malfunction in a power line not far from Diagoras's estate, several workmen tried to gain entrance to his house. At first they were unsuccessful. When they finally broke in, they found the building deserted and all the machines destroyed, except for two large copper vats that were untouched and completely empty.

I alone know what they contained, and it is precisely for that reason that I dare not make conjectures connecting those contents with the disappearance of their creator, who has not been seen since.

Let Us Save the Universe

(An Open Letter from Ijon Tichy)

After a long stay on Earth I set out to visit my favorite places from my previous expeditions—the spherical clusters of Perseus, the constellation of the Calf, and the large stellar cloud in the center of the Galaxy. Everywhere I found changes, which are painful for me to write about, because they are not changes for the better. There is much talk nowadays about the growth of cosmic tourism. Without question tourism is wonderful, but everything should be in moderation.

The eyesores begin as soon as you are out the door. The asteroid belt between Mars and Jupiter is in deplorable condition. Those monumental rocks, once enveloped in eternal night, are lit up now, and to make matters worse, every crag is carved with initials and monograms.

Eros, the particular favorite of lovers, shakes from the explosions with which self-taught calligraphers gouge inscriptions in its crust. A couple of shrewd operators there rent out hammers, chisels, and even pneumatic drills, and a man cannot find an untouched rock in what were once the most rugged areas.

Everywhere are graffiti like IT WAS LOVE AT FIRST SIGHT ON THIS HERE METEORITE, and arrow-pierced hearts in the worst taste. On Ceres, which for some reason large families like, there is a veritable plague of photography. The many photographers there don't just rent out spacesuits for posing, but cover mountainsides with a special emulsion and for a nominal fee immortalize on them entire groups of vacationers. The huge pictures are then glazed to make them permanent. Suitably posed families—father, mother, grandparents, children—smile from cliffs. This, as I read in some prospectus, creates a "family atmosphere." As regards Juno, that once beautiful planetoid is all but gone; anyone who feels like it chips stones off it and hurls them into space. People have spared neither nickel-iron meteors (which have gone into souvenir signet rings and cuff links) nor comets. You won't find a comet with its tail intact any more.

I thought I would escape the congestion of cosmobuses, the family portraits on cliffs, and the graffiti doggerel once I left the Solar System. Was I wrong!

Professor Bruckee from the observatory complained to me recently that both stars in Centaurus were growing dim. How can they not grow dim when the entire area is filled with trash? Around the heavy planet Sirius, the chief attraction of this system, is a ring like those of Saturn, but formed of beer bottles and lemonade containers. An astronaut flying that route must dodge not only swarms of meteors but also tin cans, eggshells, and old newspapers. There are places where you cannot see the stars, for all the rubbish. For years astrophysicists have been racking their brains over the reason for the great difference in the amounts of cosmic dust in various galaxies. The answer, I think, is quite simple: the higher a civilization is, the more dust and refuse it produces. This is a problem more for janitors than for astrophysicists. Other nebulae have not been able to cope with it, either, but that is small comfort.

Spitting into space is another reprehensible practice. Saliva, like any liquid, freezes at low temperatures, and colliding with it can easily lead to disaster. It is embarrassing to mention, but individuals who fall sick during a voyage seem to consider outer space their personal toilet, as if unaware that the traces of their distress will orbit for millions of years, arousing in tourists bad associations and an understandable disgust.

Alcoholism is a special problem.

Beyond Sirius I began counting the huge signs advertising Mars vodka, Galax brandy, Lunar gin, and Satellite champagne, but soon lost count. I hear from pilots that some cosmodromes have been forced to switch from alcohol fuel to nitric acid, there being nothing of the former left to use for takeoff. The patrol service says that it is difficult to spot a drunken person from a distance: people blame their staggering on weightlessness. And the practices of certain space stations are a disgrace. I once asked that my reserve bottles be filled with oxygen, after which, having traveled no more than a parsec, I heard a strange burbling and found that I had been given, instead, pure cognac! When I went back, the station director insisted that I had winked when I spoke to him. Maybe I did wink—I have a stye—but does that justify such a state of affairs?

Confusion reigns on the main routes. The huge number of accidents is not surprising, considering that so many people regularly exceed the speed limit. The worst offenders are women: by traveling fast they slow the passage of time and age less. Also, one frequently encounters rattletraps, like the old cosmobuses that pollute the length of the ecliptic with their exhaust.

When I landed on Palindronia and asked for the complaint book, I was told that it had been smashed the day before by a meteorite. And the supply of oxygen is running short. Six light-years from Beluria it cannot be obtained anywhere; people who go there to sightsee are forced to freeze themselves and wait, reversibly dead, for the next shipment of air, because if alive they would have not a thing to breathe. When I arrived, there was no one at the cosmodrome; they were all hibernating in the coolers. But in the cafeteria I saw a complete assortment of drinks—from pineapples in cognac to pilsner.

Sanitary conditions, particularly on those planets within the Great Preserve, are outrageous. In the *Voice of Mersituria* I read an article calling for the extermination of those splendid beasts, the swallurkers. These

A swallurker at night with victim

predators have on their upper lips a number of shiny warts in diverse patterns. In the last few years, however, a variety with warts arranged in the form of two zeroes has been appearing more frequently. Swallurkers usually hunt in the vicinity of campsites, where at night, under cover of darkness, they lie, with wide-open jaws, in wait for people seeking a secluded spot. Doesn't the author of the article realize that the animals are completely innocent, that one should blame not them but those responsible for the lack of proper plumbing facilities?

On this same Mersituria the absence of public conveniences has caused a whole series of mutations among insects.

In places famous for beautiful views one often sees comfortable wicker chairs that seem to invite the weary

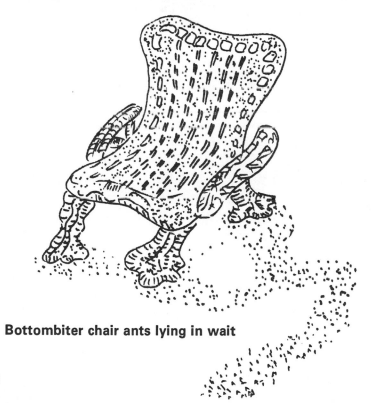

Bottombiter chair ants lying in wait

stroller. If he eagerly sits down between the arms, the supposed chair attacks, for it is actually thousands of spotted ants (the bottombiter chair ant, *Multipodium pseudostellatum Trylopii*) that group together and mimic wicker furniture. Rumor has it that certain other varieties of arthropods (fripples, scrooches, and brutalacean rollipedes) have mimicked soda stands, ham-

A brutalacean rollipede

mocks, and even showers with faucets and towels, but I cannot vouch for the truth of such assertions, having myself seen nothing of the kind, and the myrmecological authorities are silent on this point. However, I should give a warning about a rather rare species, the snakefooted telescoper (*Anencephalus pseudoopticus tripedius Klaczkinensis*). The telescoper also stations itself in scenic spots, extending its three long, thin legs like a tripod and aiming its tubular tail at the scenery. With the saliva that fills its mouth opening, it imitates the lens of a telescope, enticing the careless tourist to take a peek, with extremely unpleasant consequences. Another snake, the trippersneak (*Serpens vitiosus Reichenmantlii*), found on the planet Gaurimachia, lurks in bushes and trips unwary passers-by with its tail. However, this reptile feeds exclusively on blondes and does not mimic anything.

The universe is not a playground, nor is biological evolution an idyll. We ought to publish brochures like those I saw on Derdimona, warning amateur botanists about the cruella (*Pliximiglaquia bombardans L.*). The cruella has gorgeous flowers, but they must not be picked, because the plant lives in symbiosis with the brainbasher, a tree bearing fruit that is melon-sized and spiked. The careless botanizer need pluck only one flower, and a shower of rock-hard missiles will descend upon his head. Neither the cruella nor the brainbasher does any harm to the victim afterward; they are content with the natural consequences of his death, for it helps fertilize the surrounding soil.

But marvels of mimicry occur on all the planets in the Preserve. The savannas of Beluria, for example, abound with colorful flowers, among which there is a crimson rose of wondrous beauty and fragrance (the *Rosa mendatrix Tichiana*, as Professor Pingle named it, for I was the first to describe it). This flower is actually a growth on the tail of the herpeton, a Belurian predator. The hungry herpeton hides in a thicket, extending its extremely long tail far ahead, so that only the flower protrudes from the grass. When an unsuspecting tourist stoops to smell it, the beast pounces on him from behind. Its tusks are almost as long as an elephant's. What a strange, extraterrestrial confirmation, this, of the adage that every rose has its thorns!

If I may digress a little, I cannot help recalling another Belurian marvel, a distant relative of the potato—the sentient gentian (*Gentiana sapiens suicidalis* Pruck). The name of this plant derives from certain of its mental properties. It has sweet and very tasty bulbs. As a result of mutation, the gentian will sometimes form tiny brains instead of the usual bulbs. This mutant variety, the crazy gentian (*Gentiana mentecapta*), becomes restless as it grows. It digs itself out, goes into the forest, and gives itself up to solitary meditation. It invariably reaches the conclusion that life is not worth living, and commits suicide.

The gentian is harmless to man, unlike another Belurian plant, the furiol. This species has adapted to an environment created by intolerable children. Such children, constantly running, pushing, and kicking whatever lies in their path, love to break the eggs of the spiny slothodile. The furiol produces fruits identical in form to these eggs. A child, thinking he has an egg in front of him, gives vent to his urge for destruction and smashes it with a kick. The spores contained in the pseudo-egg are released and enter his body. The infected child develops into an apparently normal individual, but before long an incurable malignant process sets in: cardplaying, drunkenness, and debauchery are the successive stages, followed by either death or a great career. I have often heard the opinion that furiols should be extirpated. Those who say this do not stop to think that children should be taught, instead, not to kick objects on foreign planets.

I am by nature an optimist and try to have faith in man, but it is not always easy. On Prostostenesa lives a small bird known as the scribblemock (*Graphomanus spasmaticus Essenbachii*), the counterpart of the terrestrial parrot, except that it writes instead of talks. Often, alas, it writes on fences the obscenities it picks up from

A scribblemock

tourists from Earth. Some people deliberately infuriate this bird by taunting it with spelling errors. The creature then begins eating everything in sight. They feed it ginger, raisins, pepper, and yellwort, an herb that lets out a long scream at sunrise (it is sometimes used as an alarm clock). When the bird dies of overeating, they barbecue it. The species is now threatened with extinction, for every tourist who comes to Prostostenesa looks forward to a meal of roast scribblemock, reputed to be a great delicacy.

Some people believe that it is all right if humans eat creatures from other planets, but when the reverse takes place they raise a hue and cry, call for military assistance, demand punitive expeditions, etc. Yet it is anthropomorphic nonsense to accuse extraterrestrial flora or fauna of treachery. If the deadly deceptorite, which looks like a rotten tree stump, stands posing on its hind legs to mimic a signpost along a mountain trail, leads hikers astray, and devours them when they fall into a

A deadly deceptorite

chasm—if, I say, the deceptorite does this, it is only because the rangers in the Preserve do not maintain the road signs. The paint peels off the signs, which causes them to rot and resemble that animal. Any other creature, in its place, would do the same.

The famous mirages of Stredogentsia owe their existence solely to man's vicious inclinations. At one time chillips grew on the planet in great numbers, and warmstrels were hardly ever found. Now the latter have multiplied incredibly. Above thickets of them, the air, heated artificially and diffracted, gives rise to mirages of taverns, which have caused the death of many a traveler from Earth. It is said that the warmstrels are entirely to blame. Why, then, don't their mirages mimic schools, libraries, or health clubs? Why do they always show places where intoxicating beverages are sold? The answer is simple. Because mutations are random, warmstrels at first created all sorts of mirages, but those that showed people libraries and adult-education classes starved to death, and only the tavern variety (*Thermomendax spirituosus halucinogenes* of the family Anthropophagi) survived. This special adaptation of the warmstrel, brought about by man himself, is a powerful indictment of our vices.

Not long ago I was incensed by a letter to the editor in the *Stredogentsia Echo*. The writer demanded the removal of both the warmstrels and the solinthias, those magnificent trees that are the pride of every park. When their bark is cut, poisonous, blinding sap squirts out. The solinthia is the last Stredogentsian tree not carved from top to bottom with graffiti and initials—and now we are to get rid of it? A similar fate appears to threaten such valuable fauna as the vengerix, the maraudola, the morselone, and the electric howler. The latter, to protect itself and its offspring from the nerve-racking noise of countless tourist radios in the forest, has developed, through natural selection, the ability to cancel out particularly loud rock-and-roll music. The electrical organs of the howler emit superheterodyne waves, so this unusual creation of nature should be placed under protection at once.

As for the foul-tailed fetido, I admit that the odor it gives off has no equal. Doctor Hopkins of the University of Milwaukee has calculated that particularly active specimens can produce up to five kr (kiloreeks) per second. But even a child knows that the fetido does this only when photographed. The sight of an aimed camera triggers a reaction known as the lenticular-subcaudal

A foul-tailed fetido

Gauleiterium flagellans

reflex—it is nature attempting to shield this innocent creature from the intrusions of rubbernecks. Although it is true that the fetido, being rather nearsighted, sometimes takes for a camera such objects as ashtrays, lighters, watches, and even medals and badges, this is partly because some tourists use miniature cameras; it is easy to make a mistake. As for the observation that in recent years fetidos have increased their range and now produce up to eight megareeks per acre, I must point out that the cause here is the widespread use of telephoto lenses.

I do not wish to give the impression that I consider all extraterrestrial animals and plants beyond criticism. Certainly carnivamps, saprophoids, geeklings, dementeria, and marshmuckers are not particularly likable, nor are the mysophilids from the family Autarchiae, including *Gauleiterium flagellans, Syphonophiles pruritualis,* and the throttlemor (*Lingula stranguloides Erdmenglerbeyeri*). But think the matter over carefully and try to be objective. Why is it proper for a human to pick flowers and dry them in a herbarium, but unnatural for a plant to tear off and preserve ears? If the echoloon (*Echolalium impudicum Schwamps*) has multiplied on Aedonoxia beyond all measure, humans are to blame for this, too. The echoloon derives its life energy from sound. Once thunder served it as a food source; in fact, it still likes to listen to storms. But now it has switched to tourists. Each tourist treats the echoloon to a volley of the filthiest curses. It is amusing, they say, to watch the creature literally blossom under a torrent of abuse. It does indeed grow, but because of the energy absorbed from sonic vibrations, not because of the profanities shouted by excited tourists.

Where is all this leading? Such species as the blue wizzom and the drillbeaked borbit have disappeared; thousands of others are dying out. Sunspots are increasing due to clouds of rubbish. I still remember the time when the great treat for a child was the promise of a Sunday trip to Mars; but now the little monster will not

A drillbeaked borbit

eat his breakfast unless Daddy produces a supernova especially for him! By squandering nuclear energy, polluting asteroids and planets, ravaging the Preserve, and leaving litter everywhere we go, we shall ruin outer space and turn it into one big dump. It is high time we came to our senses and enforced the laws. Convinced that every minute of delay is dangerous, I sound the alarm: let us save the Universe.